Rubbing (noun): an image of a raised, incised, or textured surface obtained by placing paper over it and rubbing the paper with a colored substance.

"Rubbing." Merriam-Webster.com Dictionary, Merriam-Webster, https://www.merriam-webster.com/dictionary/rubbing. Accessed 18 Feb. 2024.

Rub (intransitive verb):

1 a: an unevenness of surface (as of the ground in lawn bowling)

b: OBSTRUCTION, DIFFICULTY

c: something grating to the feelings (such as a gibe or harsh criticism)

d: something that mars serenity

2: the application of friction with pressure

"Rub." Merriam-Webster.com Dictionary, Merriam-Webster, https://www.merriam-webster.com/dictionary/rub. Accessed 18 Feb. 2024.

Rubbings

Chris S. Witwer

Published by Felsputzer Press.

ISBN: 979-8-218-38572-9

Copyright © 2024 by Felsputzer Press. First edition.

Cover art copyright © 2024 by Barbie J. Bohlender. *Fourth of July in England*, collage with paper, acrylic paint on canvas. https://artforallforum.org

Cover design by @ricacabrex on Fiverr

Author photo by Katherine Bliss-Reilly.

Published in the United States of America. All rights reserved.

Certain oddities in punctuation, use of or lack of use quotations around dialogue, and special formatting in some stories are on purpose to create a certain feel, sound, and pacing of the words. Any typos, however, are entirely the fault of gremlins.

"When you travel you step back from your own days, from the fragmented imperfect linearity of your time. As when reading a novel, the events and people become allegorical and eternal. The boy whistles on a wall in Mexico. Tess leans her head against a cow. They will keep doing that forever; the sun will just keep on falling into the sea."

Lucia Berlin, *Luna Nueva*

"The cure for anything is salt water – sweat, tears, or the salt sea."

Isak Dinesen, *Seven Gothic Tales*

With many thanks to David Schowengerdt for his close and careful reading, and to Jennifer Morris and Shi for their encouragement and questions on early drafts of this book. Thanks too to April Laragy Stein, Jill Williamson Rogers, and Linda Zietlow for their support.

Special thanks to Barbie J. Bohlender for her love and friendship and joy and art. Back at ya.

Contents

1997

The flickering light woke me. Dark, light, dark, light.

My eyes opened to the most magnificent scene I had ever beheld. Shockingly blue Mediterranean waters. Cobalt blue under a pastel sky. Cousteau blue. A fathomless vast azure sea.

The train popped in and out of black empty tunnels and emerged again into the total opposite of black. The splendor knocked the wind right out of me before I was even fully conscious. We were high above the sea, hugging a rugged cliff. Rocks and small trees on the right, the endless Mediterranean on the left.

One of the best surprises of my life.

And I have never slept on a train again, not once.

* * *

This is the story of my trip to Europe after college, in 1997. It's my attempt at a coming-of-age story. I want to share my European experiences with you. From London, where I took quick verbal snapshots acting very much like a tourist, to Paris, where I sought out some of the most beautiful art and architecture in the world. I came to truly love Salzburg and the Italian Riviera. I spent extra time in both, allowing me to explore both internal and external landscapes.

First, imagine being in a foreign country without your phone, without any devices whatsoever. Not because they were broken or lost, but because those little computers in our pockets didn't even exist yet. Nothing did. There were no online cafés, no laptops, no tablets for checking email or reserving a bed for the night.

Six weeks alone. England, France, Austria, Italy, France again, and a day trip to Monaco. No detailed itinerary, no concrete plans. Just me and a copy of *Let's Go Europe*, a wish list (e.g., see the Louvre) and notes from a friend who had done something similar a few years before.

I would come to enjoy the fact that nobody in the entire world knew where I was. There is real beauty in such aloneness.

The trip was, of course, chronological. My mind is not. I've had all these years to revise, improve, fantasize. I am, after all, a storyteller. If you find yourself in these pages, we'll remember it differently. As we should.

This book is crafted from the travel journal I carried with me to each of the cities I visited, to each museum and café and hostel and park and train and plane… everywhere.

Twenty-five years and a course of chemo later, I re-read the journal cover to cover one Saturday morning, stretched out on a chaise with a cup of coffee. How could I have written so little about where I was, and what I was experiencing? So little about what I saw, and what I was doing?

Turns out my most lasting memories often aren't even mentioned. My hand-written journal entries hadn't yet identified the important moments. But I will tell you about them anyway.

I graduated college about 8 years later than my peers did. It was a hard haul, dropping out for both financial reasons and needing time off to refocus. When I went back, it was bit by bit while working full time. I finally walked across the stage in December of 1996. All those years of trying to become a college graduate were done. I was a first-generation college grad. What next?

A private company had offered me another student loan. I explained that I wasn't eligible, that I was graduating. They told me I could take the loan anyway, and do whatever I liked with it: car, house, travel.

Travel! I could see all the marvels I'd been reading about for years. Westminster Abbey. The Louvre. The LOUVRE!! Salzburg with its Mozart museum and Sacher-Torte and capuchin monks and

"Do-Re-Mi." The Colosseum in Rome. Long train rides, the Italian Riviera.

Europe. ME! Van Gogh paintings and the Duomo. It would be like finishing my education, in a way. Touching and breathing and thinking beyond the textbook in the tradition of so many writers who experienced Europe before me. Washington Irving, Ralph Waldo Emerson, F. Scott Fitzgerald, Gertrude Stein, Eudora Welty.

Ah, Eudora Welty.

I wasn't one of those kids who was supposed to make it to Europe. No money, no family connections, no mentors.

They didn't have to ask me twice to put myself further into debt. This was my only shot. I'd never have this kind of money or time, not once I began working and coupled up and took on whatever responsibilities my life would be made of.

I gave up my apartment, put all my things in storage, quit the job that had put me through college, and left Austin with nothing but a backpack and a shiny new Eurail pass.

Eurail Pass: $376 for 5 days for France, Italy, Germany and Austria. I'd start in London and go to Paris. From there, through Germany to Salzburg. Then down to Italy, up to the Italian Riviera, and back into France to Nice.

Plane tickets: $694 round trip flying into London and then back home out of Nice. Stops in NY City on the way out, Dallas on the way back.

Here are some of the things I did not know the day I boarded that first international flight:

- Italian and Spanish are not that similar. Knowing a little textbook Spanish won't get you far.
- The French don't sit in coffee shops writing the day away. Neither do Italians.
- How to read metro maps
- Italians don't take "no" easily. They're also incredibly loud.
- I was really out of shape.
- I had a badly injured ankle.
- Traveling alone is hard, and wonderful.
- I was about to have the time of my life.

By the end of this trip, I wanted to understand myself a bit better, to understand other people a bit better, and to learn to write. Would this trip help me find which of Frost's paths in the yellow wood were mine? Was I a writer? How would I know?

London

My family worried that the plane would crash into the ocean, and I would die. My youngest sister even called the night before my flight to come out to me. "I didn't want you to die not knowing I'm gay, too."

Thanks?

I am naturally trusting. I trusted the plane to stay in the sky. I trusted the pilots to land it safely. I trusted trains and buses to get me where I needed to go. And I trusted myself to keep my passport and money safe in my travel wallet, snugly fitted around my waist under my clothing. I really did trust myself.

The flight was amazing. The sun's pale light shimmered above the water, a near-constant almost-sunrise. Pastel colors near the horizon. Beautiful and impossible to turn away from. Warm towels at the end.

But landing at the airport at 4am local time meant no money changers, no food, no water to buy. I couldn't find a subway tunnel to take me into the city proper. I was essentially stranded, exhausted, sleepless. The tears came quickly. The first thing I did in Europe was cry. Of course.

London was supposed to be the easiest place I'd go. Similar culture, same language. But I hadn't accounted for the time change. The next surprise – the airport wasn't really in London. Trains would run later, but not yet. And I had at least an hour-long ride ahead of me.

But I noticed a group of backpackers gathered together, sitting and waiting. I joined them thinking there's safety in numbers. Eventually I found my voice and began to ask questions, right around the time everything started to open for business.

By the time I rode the train into London, took the Tube to Paddington where I would stay the night, ate, and found the hostel, I really needed sleep. Jetlag, a new experience, kicked my ass pretty hard. So there I was, my first day in London, declining some very nice hostel mates' offers to join their touring activities. One of them mentioned that I could have stayed home for a nap.

True, that.

The hostel was like a small homey B & B with a daily continental breakfast, shared bedroom and bath, quiet with owners on-site. It felt safe and normal.

BTW, Nutella. What is this magical substance??!

Refreshed, where to go first? Westminster Abbey! I'd read Washington Irving's description of it in *The Sketchbook of Geoffrey Crayon,* originally published serially in 1819 and 1820.

> "As I paced the cloisters, sometimes contemplating this mingled picture of glory and decay, and sometimes endeavoring to decipher the inscriptions on the tombstones which formed the pavement beneath my feet, my eye was attracted to three figures rudely carved in relief, but nearly worn away by the footsteps of many generations."

I sat on a stone bench looking out to the Gothic flying buttresses and enjoyed a hot, dark coffee. It was lovely. The stones held the air's coolness. The flying buttresses were prettier than I had imagined. And I picked a tiny flower – a weed probably -- from the lawn and pressed it between the pages of my journal. Somewhere I read that when you pick a flower, you're making room for another bloom.

At noon in the cathedral, the woman minister had everyone stop and pray for peace – in memory of the unknown soldier. And then we said the Lord's Prayer, which I still knew then. The building was old and smelled of centuries. I couldn't believe I was here. The tears came easily again.

There was a sign offering "rubbings" of various famous English persons, so I shelled out a few pounds and made a rubbing of Shakespeare. There was a marker for tourists to rub repeatedly until Shakespeare's raised image – the one on the marker – was transferred onto the paper. Gold crayon on thick black construction paper. What an odd tradition, rubbings. I folded the paper and put it in my pack. Shakespeare isn't buried in Westminster Abbey, but he's still present in this hallowed place.

I crossed the street to Buckingham Palace. During the Changing of the Guard, I stood alongside tourists from many nations. Buckingham Palace is huge and old. The windows fascinated me - what does it look like inside? What would it look like to stare out one of those windows? (Note to self: watch *The Crown*, streaming on Netflix, when you're older). While we cued up for the ceremony, a mounted guard kept moving people back with her horse as newcomers cut in line. She taunted those of us who hadn't complained, "You gonna let them stand in front of you? You were here first, you know. No need to be nice about it!"

Story of my life, really. Letting people cut in front of me, not complaining to them about it. I'll complain to you or grumble to myself, but I don't really like confrontation.

In a single day, I managed to see: Westminster Abbey, Changing of the Guard ceremony, Hyde Park (where I sang "MacArthur Park" at the top of my lungs, because I could), Piccadilly Circus, the National Gallery, the Tower of London, Tower Bridge, Big Ben, then to Greenwich for tea, and finally a glimpse of the beautiful, hushed, St. Paul's Cathedral. I saw them, but I didn't really absorb them. Still, I had to move fast. There was much to see before the end of my six week tour.

To get to Greenwich, which I later realized I had confused with Greenwich VILLAGE, I rode atop a red double-decker bus. Open seating on top, no roof. It went into the tunnel connecting London and the Docklands. It was very dark, and the bus went very fast. I wondered if this is where Roald Dahl got the idea for Willy Wonka's tunnel of terror boat ride. It was so fun. The wind tousled my hair from all directions, and I kept expecting images of monsters and bugs and villains and flashing red lights to appear on the tunnel walls like in the movie version.

But I wasn't done with terror-filled tunnels yet. There was an underground pedestrian tunnel between me and the tea shop I wanted to visit. That tunnel isn't underground though, it's underwater! The River Thames flows above. Which is why the water dropping from the ceiling to the floor was so utterly terrifying. I scurried along quickly.

At the shop I had my first real tea with milk and a biscuit; a satisfying English tea break. In Greenwich, on a cloudy day, cold tired feet, no tourists. I had arrived a good month before tourist season. On this trip I learned that off-season travel has its charms.

Not only is it cheaper, but there's more room, more space, more time. Fewer people.

My ankle hurt a lot after all the walking. It hadn't been too swollen when I left home, but I could feel this grinding sensation now with every step. I'd hurt it when I slipped down the concrete stairs just outside my apartment a few days before departure. My doctor thought it was sprained. No big deal. I'd bought all my tickets non-refundable so I could afford them. The ankle wasn't falling off. I'd be fine.

I dined at Garfunkel's restaurant in Paddington. Sausage, peas, mashed potatoes. The onion gravy was divine. Blackberry and apple crumble with vanilla ice cream. My midwestern palate was pleased. The tea was a lot like Dad's sun tea when it's still warm. Pickwick brand English breakfast tea. Breakfast (tea) for dinner!

London is the biggest city I'd ever seen up close. I'd seen pockets of Dallas, but nothing so *big city*. There was ugly, dilapidated housing near the train tracks between Gatwick and London proper. Poorly clothed children playing in weedy yards, stopping their games to watch the trains go by. And then in the city, so many skyscrapers. Inaccessible businesses doing who knows what behind shiny, mirrored facades, all the businesspeople dressed sharply, walking briskly, unseeing.

It's easy to feel lonely in London.

I felt like Ted Edward Bear, the star of my favorite Christmas story, *The Bear Who Slept Through Christmas*, in that scene where he finds himself stumbling under the hurried feet of rushed, self-important, well-dressed shoppers in a city full of honking horns and angry shouts.

Briefly, I was Ted E. Bear. Mouth agape, confused, lost, caught in the lights. Overwhelmed by the cacophony. Determined. I still believed in my future the way Ted believed in Santa. Opportunity. Equality. Knowledge, and the value of it. Hard work rewarded.

Now that I think about it, Santa toils alone, unrewarded, for the better part of every year. Then builds a team and goes on a brief but highly publicized tour, only to repeat the cycle again the next year. Not unlike a book tour, right?

It was time to slow down and see some art. At the National Gallery, I visited the Monet exhibit. There were young school children, 5-7 years old, sketching paintings. I watched a little girl draw Antibes. She used a regular pencil and sketched quickly, not worrying about getting it right. She used her finger to blend the sky. What beauty she has. Her enjoyment, her focus. Her pleasure was infectious. She uttered little syllables occasionally, "yes" "oh" "ah."

The Gare St. Lazare was here. And a water lily room. My favorites were *Waterlily – Sunset*, and *Flood Waters*. The colors spoke to me, evoking clarity through suggestion.

- There were teens sketching the Cézannes. Gosh, they drew well. I always wanted to draw.

- Seurat's *The Channel of Gravelines, Grand Fort-Philippe* – even the borders are points.

- Van Gogh's *Sunflowers*. Just as I had hoped they'd be. Brilliant, iconic, yellow.

- Ah! Tintoretto's *The Origin of the Milky Way*, with Zeus holding Hercules to Hera's breast. I tried to reproduce it in my journal. In pen. To this day, I crack up when I look at my sketch of Zeus putting Heracles to Athena's breast. It's a ridiculous rendering, but it does include all the main components, including the cupids. I give myself a C+

- George Michel, *Stormy Landscape with Ruins on a Plain* – the clouds are moving. How is that possible?

And then I fell in love -- JMW Turner's *Dutch Boats in a Gale*. Agitated white caps fully illuminated, as if there were not just a light shining on them, but from under and within. Where does the light come from? Why is my eye so drawn to it? Light against dark, against angry deep blue waters, under stormy clouds rushing left to right, east to west, there to here. Rushing, rushing. In the background 3 ships, one safely in the still waters under a clear sky and pale sun. Can they rescue the damned in time? Will they? And look! There's a dog. The red bandana, the terrorized passengers, the frantic crew, the old man trying to stay in the hull that will surely capsize with the next gush or gust or gale. One picture. One frame. The waves at eye level, the boat about to dump its passengers directly into my line of sight. So much. I have fallen in love with so much.

Next up, a visit to 221B Baker Street, the site of Sherlock's pub. Tonic and lime, a cigarette, and then a nice local man took my picture for my scrapbook.

Harrods was a wonder. All I could afford was a cassette tape: Elgar's *Symphony #2* – I have it still, even though I no longer have a cassette player. I love Elgar. I was in the symphonic band in high school, where we played Elgar's *Enigma Variations*. Love love love.

In Harrod's café, I ordered an apple brie sandwich. I did not enjoy the brie at all, but 25 years later I remember that unusual sandwich with the hard crusty bread, tart apple, and thick, cold stab of brie cheese. Money well spent.

There's a lesson here – not all expenditures bring happiness or pleasure or even satisfaction – but they can still be a great buy.

At the Victoria & Albert Museum, I wandered about as long as my ankle would allow. The Frank Lloyd Wright miniature was fantastic. They had Kaufman's office set up in there, everything down to the Diego Rivera painting. I loved that wall, the designs in the wooden wall. And the desk from Johnson Wax was cool too.

Another night, another dinner out. When in London, order the fish and chips.

The pub was named after the St. Osyth dragon which was mentioned in a broadside - a proclamation - of 1704. It says, "Before Henry II died, a dragon of marvelous bigness was discovered at St. Osyth in Essex."

There were puddings on the dessert menu, and I didn't have any idea what an English pudding was, so I asked the waitress about the most interestingly named pudding, "What's the spotted dick?"

"Dessert," she said. Fair enough. I ordered it.

My whirlwind tour of London was over. I would leave London underground, underwater, via the Eurostar. We moved fast in the dark, occasionally lit tunnel beneath the English Channel. An enclosed tube barreling its way to Paris. Nothing like the double-decker and its tunnel. I sat at a small table facing an opposing passenger, a young businessman reading the papers. We smoked our cigarettes and nodded periodic acknowledgements of one another whenever our eyes met on the 2-hour trip to Paris' Gare du Nord.

Paris

Paris doesn't have an ocean, though it sure would be grand if it did. The City of Lights with sand and coastal skies and sea breezes that whisk away the acrid odors of Parisian life: cigarettes, moldering buildings, sex, fish guts.

Paris. Oh Paris, what a dream I had of Paris. That I'd find small quiet coffee shops with wooden counters (found those) and baristas as skilled as bar men (found those too!) and sit (nope!) and write all day (nope!), while café staff smiled knowingly at me (LOL, no).

That's not how Paris works. If you want to sit, order a full meal with friends or family. If you want a quick coffee, expect to chug a pull of espresso then go on your way. Sitting and espresso don't really go together.

Paris was fairly quiet that first morning, a Sunday. I began walking early, past the little market next to the hostel, past a street vendor washing fish guts into the gutter with a garden hose. Paris is pretty smelly, even without the fish gut guy. I walked along nibbling a crusty baguette. From the hostel through residential areas to the Eiffel Tower, then to the Arc de Triomphe, stopping to peer into small courtyards and playgrounds, hoping to catch glimpses of Parisian life.

The Eiffel Tower. By the time I got to it, there was a ridiculously long line. The ticket price to ride the elevator up was pretty steep. I'd really just wanted to see the tower itself, not so much the view from the top of it. So I found a bench in the Eiffel Tower's shadow and people-watched from the beautifully maintained Champ de Mars, a lovely tree-lined park still damp with dew that morning.

It was at that moment that I wondered if my Walkman radio would work outside the U.S. I'd brought it to Europe just in case, and it was in my day pack. I turned it on. You'll never guess the first song I heard coming out of my little headphones?

"Born in the U.S.A."

That was a good laugh, it really was. I need more of those laughs in my life.

By the time I got to the Arc de Triomphe, there was a lot of traffic. Cars flying around the traffic circle that separated me from the Arc. I didn't know much about that landmark, only the brief paragraph written in my guidebook, but I knew if I walked down the Champs-Elysees to the other Arc, I'd find some of the best art in the world.

Destination: Louvre.

The Champs-Elysees was lined with gleaming silver, shiny glass, impossibly tall buildings. The window displays were stunning, showing off fashion and products I would never in my life be able to afford – probably not even the knockoffs. That's ok. I could see them, imagine what it was like to want them. I didn't. I was wearing sneakers, overalls (so, no bra!). There was a 3 story McDonalds, shiny, fully packed with tourists and only a handful of locals. Small budget, I got a small snack. Sacrilege I regretted immediately. When in Paris, why the hell go to McDonald's? Comfort, I suppose. Curiosity.

Walking the Champs-Elysees was pretty special. Such luxury. High end everything. Just a few months later, Laduree would open their Champs-Elysees location, so I missed that then but I do now live near one in Maryland. Of all things. I suppose those macarons in Paris are 1,000 times better than those made in the U.S. using American egg whites, flours, and sugars. Like gelato in Italy is 3,000 times better than any gelato you can buy in the U.S. no matter how authentic the recipe, no matter how Italian the gelateria is.

I actually missed macarons altogether while in France. Tragic. I did not know what a macaron was, and I did not taste a single one on this trip. (I did, however, become a fan of the mille-feuille so don't feel too sorry for me.)

Later, at home in Austin, I would watch on television as the peloton cycled around and past the Arc de Triomphe in the final stage of the Tour de France. An Austin hero for a time, Lance Armstrong, giving the whole world something to cheer about together. And then again, and again, and again... and every year I watched that race, I remembered standing there with the cars whizzing by, not sure how to get to the Arc to touch it, see it up close, stand in its shadow. But it didn't matter. I had seen Paris.

I walked and walked. Clean wide flat sidewalks, young trees with new green leaves making tiny shade. A gentle breeze. An old man wearing a half-buttoned cardigan and a trilby sauntered past me going the opposite direction, taking in the cool morning. I wondered about his life.

I walked the entire Champs-Elysees from the Arc de Triomphe to the Louvre, stopping to ogle small wares sold on blankets overlooking a garden where people sat in chairs. They sat. In chairs. Scores of them, just sitting. I sat with them for a time.

We could use more of that at home. Just sitting, thinking, resting, talking, reading, soaking up the sun.

I was still disappointed that Paris doesn't have coffeehouses and bars you can sit and write novels in for hours, as I had expected. I guess I was a little spoiled by Austin's college culture but even so, I knew Hemingway enjoyed cafes. Didn't Sartre meet Simone de Beauvoir at a café? Actually, didn't a lot of artists gather at Les Deux Magot in particular? I would find my way there. But in the meantime, I wanted just to get off my feet, jot a few notes or impressions in my travel journal, and enjoy a warm drink and a bready snack. No.

Every place I stopped in the heart of the city, Parisians stood up to drink their espresso, then left. Like the British pubs where everybody drinks standing up. Why couldn't I just whip out pen and paper and consume caffeine? I found a place with small tables, but they shooed me out fairly quickly. (I understand the advent of laptops has changed this quite a lot since I was there, that Parisians now loiter with electrical sockets nearby.)

Paris makes you think about how big it is. The architecture is just… people are small, we really are. I'd never been anywhere like this. The Champs-Elysée, the Louvre, Notre Dame Cathedral, everything is huge. And much of it is older than anything I'd ever seen before – though later, I'd experience the Colosseum and the Pantheon. And the ruins, where I did sit down on a low wall and write (finally!).

Paris has a complexity and a history that just doesn't exist in America. I felt this in London as well, but nowhere near as deeply. Except maybe at Westminster Abbey, when doing the Shakespeare rubbing.

Shakespeare. While thinking about Shakespeare, I got caught in a protest march of Parisian doctors, calling for improvements to their socialized medicine – I think. It was all in French. But they were passionate and wearing white coats, some with fake blood smattered across their clothes, stethoscopes, and signs with words like 'santé' – which I know now means health. Maybe a hundred of them marched in the middle of the street, chanting, staying within the boundaries the police held them to. No harm, just some traffic backups across the arrondissement.

One afternoon I went to see a movie, *The English Patient*, because it was long and indoors, and I was cold and tired and just wanted to chain smoke in a theater like I heard you could. But no, not by the time I was there in 1997. A shame, really. I was smoking Gauloises by then, the powder blue pack. Hard on the throat and lungs, but French. Smoking them allowed me to hang on to the boxed Marlboros I carried with me, which could come in handy at some point. You never know. One of my high school teachers had traded blue jeans for military belt buckles and boots on a trip to Russia.

Paris is loud. A busy place full of people doing their own thing. Unlike Italy's special kind of loud - yelling loud – which I would experience later on.

I had romanticized Paris so much in my imagination. There would be mimes and painters and poets and short men in striped shirts playing accordions on the street (there are, but only where the tourists look for them, and the point is to give them money so they can keep doing it).

Had I read *The Hunchback of Notre Dame* yet? No, I didn't read it until October of '98, according to my excel spreadsheet. I've been keeping a list of every book I've read since before college. I call it the "Repertoire" like musicians call the list of music they know and can perform. A friend once complained that my book list was all about my ego. Duh. Still is. Which is how I know that I did not read *Hunchback* until I got home – I wish I could remember. It must've been a richer read, having been inside those walls, seen its towering heights, heard the creaking wooden benches, watched the flicker of candles against the old shadows.

Since you're reading this now, you know what happens to Notre Dame later. How that beautiful, historic cathedral – that human achievement worthy of such awe - is forever changed. Again.

It was a crazy long day, and I loved it.

After seeing the Eiffel Tower and the Arc de triomphe, walking down the Champs Elysee, then around the Louvre to Notre Dame, I crossed the Seine to Shakespeare and Company - the most famous used bookstore anywhere, then spent 2 hours lost, looking for Les Deux Magot. I'd dreamt so much of writing where Sartre wrote – in a cool quiet dark cafe.

Well, Les Deux Magot was not that. It is where he met Simone De Beauvoir. I could see that, yes. But writing? Probably not, not unless the place has just become something entirely different after it became a tourist destination. When I arrived in the evening, the place was packed. I had a small table by the kitchen where I enjoyed the constant clatter of plates and glasses and bottles. Commerce, noise.

I wanted to take a matchbook home with me. A souvenir. I'd already collected a few in England, and wanted to collect more, display them in a big glass jar in my home someday, a conversation piece.

No! The grumpy, balding, harried, middle aged waiter was emphatic. No, he would not give me matches.

I put my cigarettes on the table next to the ashtray.

"No! No matchbook!" He stormed off, balancing dirty plates in the crook of his arm.

I had heard about this somewhere. Maybe at the hostel. They don't like to give matchbooks out, especially not to random American tourists who likely won't be back, and who aren't even racking up a bar tab. But I also knew someone who had succeeded in getting one and taking it home. I'd seen it. Little wooden matches in a yellow cover. She was a lot cuter and a lot flirtier than I, though. I exhaled, took a sip of coffee, and wrote something in my journal. And that's when the younger waiter who'd been flitting around behind the older guy breezed by and dropped one on my table. He didn't stop, but he gave me his killer smile over his shoulder as he moved past. I quickly put it in my pocket so Mr. Grumpy didn't see it. And later, like, twenty years later, I wondered if this was just the routine. Good cop, bad cop. Who knows.

I left a better tip than I otherwise would have.

I had already read Gertrude Stein's *Autobiography of Alice B. Toklas*, but not Hemingway's *A Moveable Feast*. That came later, after I had walked some of those same streets and written a few words at Les Deux Magot. What I wouldn't give to attend dinners like those Gertrude and Alice hosted.

Many years later I found myself responsible for the library in our office at a California university. I suggested having afternoon book discussions, a "salon" of sorts. My colleagues assumed I wanted to do nails. Sometimes I just don't fit in.

I would find other readers and writers and artists though, to drink and dine with throughout my life.

As my family used to say when insulting someone, "like seeks like." Yes. Like seeks like.

I was so sore after all that walking. The line to the Louvre was long. I didn't even know if I'd get inside before the day's end, and if I did, whether I'd have time to actually see anything. I had a list, thanks to the last elective course I took before graduation, *History of Western Art*.

#1 on the list – the sculpture *Eros and Psyche*. Then *Mona Lisa*. Picasso, Van Gogh, it was a long list.

I must've stood in the long line in front of the glass pyramid on just one foot thanks to my throbbing ankle because eventually a kind man tapped me on the shoulder. He seemed to be just walking through, not standing in the line himself. In front of me were some raucous youths jostling and poking each other, hanging on to one another laughing. Behind me, a tight-lipped American family, parents and two teens all sullen and unhappy. The man who tapped me on the shoulder spoke English to me, "Parisians, like me, we use the other entrance. Much shorter line, just around that corner over there. You will get in right away." He pointed, smiled at me, and went on his way. It was a gamble. What if he was wrong? What if he was just fucking with me as people sometimes do for no reason? What if he was a homophobe or hated Americans? While I weighed my options, the family behind me started to chitter and laugh, and ran right to where he'd pointed. They must've overheard. Gleeful, they ran past me.

They'd get there before me, but at least I wouldn't get lost. I hobbled after them, and yes, the line was shorter, quicker, the staff were friendly and helpful. The locals' entrance was the bomb.

Then I realized I was inside. In the Louvre! That magical place. So many bodies pushing past, so many languages and hurried feet. Looking up, there was glass. Was I under the pyramid? Before I could even tell, I was whisked along by a stream of people heading toward the Great Hall.

Great, the word didn't mean much to me until that very minute. Great.

The Winged Victory of Samothrace, also known as *The Winged Nike*. Nobody was even stopping to gaze upon her. I did. But not for long. The throngs of visitors kept moving. Like a slightly orderly Black

Friday shopping spree. But I saw her. Magnificent. Is she standing on a ship's prow? No, probably not. She's been here, headless, towering, majestic, atop the main staircase since 1884. Unfathomable. 1884. Where is her head? I wonder how many people have searched for it, and for how long.

In the Louvre, anything is possible. The Louvre has everything, it is everything. Birth and Death. Beginning and End. Humanity's stories, whether they comfort or scold or teach or inspire or frighten or warn or entertain. War and beauty. From the ancient civilizations to, eventually, Banksy (unofficially). Passion and crime and love and every myth there ever was. Sisyphus, the Garden of Eden, Newton's apples. Cake and caskets, ruffles and violins. Picnics and coy smiles, mirrors of every kind. Desperate ships on the verge of historical wrecking. It's all there. Rooms and rooms of portraits of the wealthy, as well as the destitute. Elite, comfortable, downtrodden, forgotten.

Clowns. There are even clowns.

I am astounded such a place as the Louvre exists. Humans are often too greedy and too lazy for such an endeavor.

I got to see the most famous painting ever – the *Mona Lisa* – in the Salle des Estats room. It's so tiny! I couldn't believe how small it is, with its outsized reputation and influence in the art world. Holy cow, it is so tiny, and the room was so packed shoulder to shoulder people pushing one another, stabbing each other with extended elbows such that I was lucky to see her at all. I didn't think I got a good photo – and wouldn't know until the roll of film was developed state-side, so I bought an official postcard of the painting in the museum gift shop. Postcards are often better than any photo I could have taken with my snapshotting Kodak.

The colors throughout the room were surprisingly rich, the lighting like gentle beacons toward the Mona Lisa and all the other beauty in that room that nobody was looking at. It made me think of beautiful women. We all look at just the one, the one we all deem most beautiful, and we stop looking right around us for any other signs of divinity.

I saw Ingres' *Oedipus Answers the Puzzle*. Gericault's *Raft of the Medusa*.

Eros and Psyche, formally *Psyche Revived by a Kiss* – sculpture by Antonio Canova, 1793 -- took my breath away, quite literally. A masterpiece like no other. How is such beauty, marked forever in stone, even possible? The sculpture is about shoulder high to me, even wider. It was in a corner, in a hall connecting other rooms. It was a surprise to find it here, amongst other sculptures, shining alabaster. The pictures never show the perfection, the detail, on the backs of those wings. You could walk around it, so I did, as did two other visitors with their cameras – one, a Japanese man who never took the viewfinder from his eye, who couldn't breathe any more than I could. We were revived, too, when next we drew breath.

Reluctantly, I stopped slowly circling *Eros and Psyche*. Reluctantly because I knew I'd never see it again. But I was actually wrong about that. I've seen it often since in my mind's eye, in reproductions, in books. It's the kiss that never ends, the one that stays with us.

Found Paul Delaroche's *The Young Martyr*. 1855, Romantic like some of my favorite music. Dramatic, passionate, reflective.

Delacrois' *Liberty Leading the People* (one day I will see *Les Mis* and the barricades would remind me of this, perhaps the fight did too.).

Devries *Mercury and Psyche.*

I looked for *Achilles and Ajax Playing a Board Game*, wandering through room after room of vases and ancient relics and jewelry and other urns. I was a little heartbroken, not being able to find it. (One day I would have the Internet in my pocket, but not yet.)

Why weren't these rooms as packed as the Salle des Estats room?

Everywhere else, the Louvre was way too crowded to relax and take notes. I spent the majority of my time looking at Greek and Roman and Italian sculpture. There was a Greek war memorial with names engraved on it from 500 BCE. It reminded me of the Vietnam memorial and how we really are much more like our ancestors than we realize.

Another tragedy of the Louvre - not staying the full day, or the week. Not staying in part due to the crowds who were. I'd seen such beauty, though. More than I could actually take in. It was like sitting in front of the ocean, unable to really process the fact that you're sitting in front of the ocean.

I wandered into a restaurant with a menu du jour (menu of the day) for only 88 francs and pointed at things on the menu that I wouldn't dare try to pronounce. I had no idea what I was ordering. They served me a nice salad with fresh little greens that looked almost like oversized clover on top of a bed of sliced beets. Beef kabobs, excellent fries, and it came with wine, but I switched that for water. The maître d brought a tall wine-shaped bottle of mineral water, took the top off, and poured it into my glass. Nice touch. I'd never been treated this way before.

Afterward, a café (espresso in a tiny little cup) and then off to the D'Orsay just 3 blocks away.

Musee d'Orsay. The building is so cool, a former train station, with levels you can walk around and the inside is open, everything light and ornate. Words fail me. Go to the Internet, you won't be disappointed.

- I saw Manet's *Le Dejeuner sur l'herbe* - a dream picnic, exactly how I envisioned the French enjoying their leisure time years ago. Except the nakedness, that surprised me a little. It used to be called *The Bath*. That makes sense.

- Whistler, *Portrait de La Mère*. And I thought I knew stern.

- Monet's *Bateaux de Plaisance* reminded me of sailboat races I watched in Florida.

- Van Gogh as he saw himself once, once upon a time.

- Cézanne too.

- Isidore Pils, *La mort d'une soeur de charité* which means, the death of the sister of charity. The light on certain people in the painting really draws your eye to them. You know where the painter wanted you to look.

So many more, I just drank it all in. No more notetaking, just looking. Really looking. I read once that people read the cards next to paintings first, then look at the painting. Not me. I look at the painting first, absorb it, study it even if briefly, then look at the cards for dates and names and any explanation included. The art comes first.

Back at the hostel, I spoke to a Taiwanese/French woman named Katerine. She's a documentary filmmaker. She asked what Chris is short for. Then she said her last heartbreak was named Chris, but it was short for the man's name. So I told her that Grandpa calls me Christopher. We'd already been talking about how people in the States (but not Europe, not yet) call me 'sir.' So she asked me "how does it feel to be part man, part woman?" I told her I am a woman. She knew that, but what she wanted to know is how it feels being treated ½ male, ½ female. I told her it hurts sometimes. Sometimes a lot, at least while I was still young. Later, it wouldn't matter much at all.

I went to Montmartre (I think!) for lunch and had a salad & croque monsieur (ham and cheese on toasted bread). Like a Stouffer's pizza without tomato sauce. Delicious.

I have this exhilarating feeling – no one in the entire world knows where I am. No one knows what I'm doing today.

Paris sure is noisy. Or maybe I am just irritable. I am still searching for a small, quiet café, but I haven't found one yet. There is, though, a tiny little bar on Rue de Vaugirard, near my hostel, the Aloha. Maybe I'll go there later.

Well, I've been called Monsieur (sir) now so I was just kidding myself. Maybe I was also kidding myself in London. Or maybe I was lucky.

So why does being "1/2 man 1/2 woman" bother me so much? Why does it feel shaming? Why can't I just accept who I am and be at peace with myself? Yes, I am part man and part woman. Everyone is. Sometimes when I look in the mirror, I really like who I see there. I did yesterday. Why does my outside affect my insides so much? No, that's not how it is. Why do others' judgements, their opinions, their assumptions, matter so much to me? How do I protect that vulnerable part of me?

Can love be a moat?

Again with the café search. All the walking really inflamed the ankle, and I decided to spend the day writing. That's part of why I was here anyway, wasn't it? To figure out how to write a novel?

Well, I found a little tiny bar in the bad part of town. Real bad. It was tiny, and quiet, and dark. I could've sat there all day. Really, I could have. But the minute I walked in, I knew it was not a place to stay. The men inside – all men – stopped talking & just stared at me. Unfriendly staring. A few whispered to one another and laughed, cackled. Crap. I had no idea what they were saying.

I ordered a coffee just to use the restroom before going on my way. The bartender pointed me to a door, through which was a dirt alley, and a hole in the ground with a door. Ick. And of course, I'd left my wet wipes at the hostel. They sure would've come in handy here.

The café was full of old men - locals who seemed shocked I'd even walked inside. I swear I heard one of them say "what is that?"

Where on earth was I? A student I worked with in Austin had recommended this neighborhood to me, but I didn't really understand his directions very well & they were partially in French so I'd either made a big mistake, or he had been trying to show me the Paris the tourists never see.

Time to chug my espresso and get the hell out of here. I should probably go back to the Seine, to where the tourists are. It felt safer. I was afraid to pull out my tourist guide on the street to even figure out how to get back there.

Right before I finished downing the thickest, harshest espresso I've ever managed to slug back, one of the truly old men in the room walked up to me, took my elbow, and steered me toward the door. He kept saying things in French but would stop and say "go" and "no" in between phrases. I grabbed my day pack from under the barstool I sat on and let him lead me into the sunlight outside. He was slow and gimpy. This clearly was hard for him, and he kept looking back over his shoulder to the door we'd just left. We walked toward some increasingly loud and violent-sounding police activity. He stopped at a cross street. Held up a few fingers, pointed. TRAIN, he said.

Got it. 3 blocks that way to the train. Get the hell out of here.

I thanked him, partly bowing, partly skipping away, grateful for the escort. To this day, I wonder what the other patrons were planning to do to me there. Rob me? Probably. They may've expected me to have a passport on me, which I did, but not in my bag. I had a money belt, and I was wearing loose overalls. The overalls felt safer than pants and a shirt, but it would only take one person to distract me and another to stick an arm down the front of the overalls for my passport and travel cheques to be at risk.

A few minutes later at the metro station a filthy, hot, crappy-looking train pulled up. I couldn't have been happier to see it.

The next day I made a brief trip to Sacre Coeur and visited the basilica. What an elegant, beautiful edifice with its organ and panoramic views. Stunning that places like this exist at all, let alone that I could pass a little time there.

Then I had a cup of coffee at the base of the stairs leading up to it. So many stairs! I walked through an outdoor market on the way down the hill, finding a fantastic black and gold PARIS t-shirt that I would be photographed in throughout the trip. It dripped black ink and fell apart the first time I put it in a real washing machine at home. Still, worth it.

I was in so much pain that I went to the hostel to lie down. They would only let me sit in the lobby because the rooms were being cleaned. After an hour I felt better and went for a walk and then to the little café/bar down the street for a croque monsieur and a café au lait. Ironically, I didn't write.

Whenever I got new roommates at the hostels, I told myself things like "they think you're a freak" or "they're afraid of you." Just because I have shorter hair than most women, and I prefer men's clothes. That's it, though. Why do I feel so different? Maybe it's my social status they're afraid of – some of them have Gucci bags. And Neutrogena face cleanser. For them, this trip is an expected rite of passage, paid for by someone else, possibly even including work or internships to launch their careers. They have studied lots of languages, some of them, and they know exactly what careers they'll be choosing. They are amazed at some of the things I say. Two girls from Antwerp thought it hilarious that I chose Spanish as my foreign language in school. Spanish being "useless." I tried to tell them it's pretty useful if you live in Texas. They didn't care. They kept giggling. I suspect the giggling was about more than the language choice.

I had been crying a lot. It felt like one giant release. All the tears I've always held back were making their way out of me now. What would they leave room for? Who would I be?

When I came to Paris, I wanted to sit and write lovely things all day. Perhaps profound things. Or stories or write a book. Not yet. I needed this experience. The pen will follow.

I had no trouble finding the Gare de Paris-Est where I'd hop a train to Germany, then transfer to another train headed to Austria. The building was stately and aged. But as I approached the entrance, my heart froze. A green clad soldier with red beret, holding a machine gun in front of his body, finger near the trigger, the barrel pointed just beyond his right foot. Is something happening? Why was he here? Can I pass by?

Of course I could, everyone else was.

I'd never seen an assault weapon before. Nor a stationed, armed soldier. I was shaken by it. What was this man protecting? Was he protecting me – a passenger? Or protecting the transit system FROM passengers like me? I didn't understand and scurried away through the long bustling halls, through the busy concourse, down to the platforms (so many!) to my train. Proud moment, navigating such an extensive transit station in a foreign country. I felt Big City. World Traveler.

Had it only been a week? Slightly more, but yes. A week and a lifetime.

Salzburg

The train ride from Paris to Munich was fun. My Eurail pass was first class, so the seats were great and the views of the French countryside were amazing. This is a travel pleasure I will discover over and over again in my life. From Washington State ferries to plane rides over the deserts of Mexico to ride shares across San Francisco – let others drive.

As night fell there were fewer and fewer people aboard and I fell asleep and I didn't wake up when we got to Munich. A railway security guard woke me by banging his flashlight against the window I was leaning against, snoring.

On the next train, a Croatian gardener gave me a Coca-Cola and a Marlboro. Universal language – smoke and a Coke. He spoke a little English and we drew pictures and made gestures to communicate. We talked, or tried to, for quite a while. Then suddenly he pointed up excitedly, up at the overhead speakers – "Salzburg! Salzburg!" I was about to miss my stop! I jumped off in the nick of time, thankfully, and found myself at 2am alone in a darkened, shut down Salzburg. Quiet, quaint, small.

No hostels this late at night. I didn't have any reservations in Salzburg because I hadn't known when I'd get there. Near the train station were a few high-end hotels whose names I recognized, but I had to ring a bell to get the staff's attention. Salzburg was shut up tight at this hour. I paid way too much for a small sleeping closet. There was no space along the side of the bed, the room was so small! But there was a dresser at the foot of the bed, and a small tv that played terrible, dubbed US TV reruns (*Tool Time*). And there was a bathtub. I soaked in it for hours, washing off the grime of the planes and trains and big cities I'd just spent the last week in.

As luck would have it, the next day I found the perfect hostel called St. Sebastian. Totally quiet, immaculately clean. $16 a night including showers, breakfast (Nutella!), lockers and kitchen access. No lockout. I could stay all day. Actually, it was a dorm, and most students were on break.

Salzburg is amazing. A dream.

First, the Zorn Witwer motorcycle company. I had read John Irving's *World According to Garp*, and then *A Prayer For Owen Meany*, and then had systematically gone back to read all the rest of his novels – including the first, *Setting Free the Bears*. Not the best first novel I'd ever read, but getting from there to *Owen Meany* was quite the feat. Anyway, in that first novel, I found reference to the Zorn-Witwer motorcycle company of Austria. So, maybe there were Witwers in Salzburg.

I went to a payphone, pulled down the hefty phone book. There were no Witwers (nor Vitvers) in the phone book. Was the motorcycle company even real? Did Witwers come from here? Or from Vienna where Irving studied? I've never liked my name before but here people think I'm German – and I do look it – it's almost like I belong. Or at least blended in. But when I handed cashiers my credit card, the clerks often giggled. My last name, it means widower. Funny ha ha.

On my way to the payphone, I'd noticed a woman and her young son, pausing to appreciate a window display of intricate Faberge-style eggs. He might've been 3 or 4 years old. He lingered and she didn't hurry him along. She waited patiently, enjoying watching him appreciate the little pieces of art. I got the sense she was just letting his brain do what kids' brains do. Why don't we do more of that at home?

At the Pamini Arabian café, the radio was playing "Top of the World" by the Carpenters.

Then outside on the street, more David Hasselhoff. If I have to hear David Hasselhoff singing one more time... what is wrong with these people? There is so much culture here. Such terrific music. What are they doing???

I had coffee with a girl named Neila, from Toronto. She's like me, traveling alone to explore herself. We took a hilarious and cheesy *Sound of Music* tour together. It was a dream come true for both of us. We sat in the back of the tour bus, giggling at the older couples up front who were singing along to the soundtrack the tour guide played for us as we passed through those hills, the hills that were so alive.

As we approached the Palace at Leopoldskron (where the children were filmed canoeing and falling into the placid green lake in rompers Maria had fashioned out of colorful drapery), our tour guide told us about being a child in World War II. When Black American soldiers would offer the Austrian children chocolate bars because the children were not afraid of Black men.

Just let that soak in.

Those Black soldiers sometimes deserted rather than go back to the U.S. Or they came back later, to live in a place where they were treated more humanely.

Neila and I took one another's pictures in front of the famous glass gazebo. The refrain from "Sixteen Going on Seventeen" came to mind. The gazebo was locked thank goodness or I might've tried to run around it on the benches as Leisl had.

I thought of my mom. She loved the musical. She must've seen it in a theater in 1965 when it came out; before she had kids, before there was a husband. We watched it every year of my childhood, all three kids on the floor in front of the television set while my parents sat on the couch behind us. We knew the words, we had the album. A wholesome, annual ritual I came to love. And this is why I wanted to see Austria. So I did.

I spent two of my six weeks in Salzburg. In the quiet. Walking, writing, thinking, looking around, seeking out Mozart's former home, reading gravestones, visiting churches. Seeking out the Capuchin monks.

The people were different, and so was the pace. This is where I invented my muse, Claire, whom I would imagine I was writing to or about or with – I was never sure. The name means "clarity" and that, that is something I wanted. Clarity. Like the clear waters, clean air, blue skies, of Salzburg.

I stayed in Old Town, where the tourists like to stay, with the carless cobblestone streets, open plazas, street musicians playing violin or cello or trumpet – classical street musicians. I met people and did things with them. I had long conversations and saw the Hale-Bop comet as I leaned out a dorm window with an opera major.

Salzburg was the first place I went around trying the same dessert at different restaurants. I still do it. There may not be a Boston Cream Pie in Boston that I haven't tried, though the one I loved the most is now gone. Durgin-Park, which opened when? 1700's? The only time I've ever entertained the thought that I might've survived in previous centuries was when tasting the Boston cream pie at Durgin-Park. And the Yankee pot roast.

In Salzburg, it was the Sacher-Torte and Mozart balls.

There were days my budget only allowed baguette and Nutella in the hostel's breakfast nook, buttered pasta I made in the hotel/dorm kitchen, and then I could treat myself to an afternoon slice of cake and a strong coffee at a local sit-down tableclothed establishment. The afternoon cakes were everything. All of them. If experiencing pleasure extends life, these saucers of chocolate heaven added decades to mine.

I wanted to buy a Tyrolean hat. Salzburg had many hat shops. Yet I knew I'd somehow crush or lose it before getting home, so I didn't dare.

I went to Mozart's birthplace, and the residence he occupied in Salzburg, then found a small but very busy music shop nearby and bought some piano music to take home:

- *Salzburger Klavierbüchlein von Wolfgang Amadeus Mozart.* Piano booklet from Salzburg.

- *Die Kleinen Klavierftude, Johann Sebastian Bach.* Minuets. Some attributed to Anna, some attributed to Wilhelm.

Another tragedy of my trip – no booze. I had decided not to drink while traveling alone in Europe, safer that way and cheaper. Which is what makes it tragic. I could've tasted so many things. So many wines!

In the mornings I watched a couple of silver-haired men in the plaza playing chess with giant knee-high chess pieces, rubbing their chins, contemplating their next moves. Not unlike me, really. Rubbing my chin, contemplating my next move.

I visited churches for historical or architectural reasons – not yet understanding the role that art plays in the church. In Salzburg, there was the Salzburg Cathedral, the Dom, with its five pipe organs, including one that has been there since 1703. Astounding. It survived the war, though barely.

There's another church whose memory is stronger for me. The postcard I kept calls it St. Andra, but today their website calls it "Andrae church." The remarkable thing about the church is a sculpture hanging on the wall behind and beside the pulpit. It took my practically-atheist breath away.

A withered stone Jesus, mounted on a wooden cross, head hung off to one side as if he was unable to hold it up any longer. Above him a figure I interpreted to be the head of god, whose hands were holding the cross just below where Jesus' hands were nailed into it. Like the father was helping hold the cross up, or standing behind his son, or just being there as part of the sacrifice. Whatever this art intended to convey to worshippers, to me it conveyed peace. There was a small angel figure below the feet too, which I at first thought was a dove. Peace. And there was a wooden circle, almost like a Venn diagram's overlap where both Jesus and the Father are together in the circle, as one.

I've never found the crucifixion story the least bit comforting, it's a horror story that entirely nullifies the term "omnipotent" in my mind. But here, this art – and the stone figures so pale and slim, not overbearing, somehow felt comforting. This was the only image or story involving a man hung on a cross that has ever done anything but scare, sadden, or anger me.

Jesus wasn't alone. Maybe we aren't either.

I sat on one of the beautifully polished wooden pews of St. Andra. I appreciated the very slight creak as I sat, I breathed in the silence of that small white room. So sparse compared to the Cathedral and other ornate and ostentatious – albeit stunning – rooms of worship. This one actually inspired quiet contemplation, more so than even Notre Dame. I just sat there breathing deeply, considering the love and care that had gone into creating this space. What these people must be like, the people who come here on Sundays together, I couldn't imagine. But I'm pretty sure they were kinder and more loving than judgmental Christians I'd known.

I'd been angry at god since 1981, when a friend's mother was killed in a car accident that changed my life. You can't experience trauma like that and just get over it. It changes you. Why did god let her die? Why did god hurt her daughter so badly? And me, why wouldn't I ever play piano in the international Van Cliburn competition, the Olympics of classical piano? Why so much pain? Why any of it.

I hadn't read Mel White's *Stranger at the Gate* yet in 1997. It was published in 1994, but my journal indicates I was still "letting go and letting god" and praying for specific things, even as I planned to return home from Europe. When I later met Dr. White at a church in Austin, he told me god said I was on the right path. Which for me was a path to being a non-believer entirely.

I was on a path, and sometimes on that path there are churches. And the people who believe in them.

* * *

I thought of my grandmother that night after I saw the churches. Grandma Polly. She taught me to sing "Jesus Loves Me." She taught me to eat gooseberry pie, and to pick cherries, to put table sugar in a glass of Pepsi, and to feed the wild cats our dinner scraps. She took me to Sunday School. And to Summer Revival, which tastes of Tootsie Rolls in my memories.

She listened to me talk and talk and talk, for hours, while we sat outside under the big shade tree shelling peas or shucking corn. We'd watch the clouds, talk about their shapes and make up stories. I loved my time alone with her, I really did.

Sometimes my sisters and I spent evenings at her house. My grandfather would come in from the farm, dirty hands, dusty overalls. He'd wash up and we'd have dinner on the Formica-topped table with metal trim. Afterwards Grandma would play Go Fish or Old

Maid on that same table with us. Maybe we'd make felt refrigerator magnets in the shape of peacocks. The proceeds went to the church's missionary fund. Sometimes she had a large bag of empty envelopes from those same missionaries. We would take the stamps off & save them in a scrapbook. Places the missionaries were visiting. We didn't know how to pronounce all the places, but we dreamed of traveling one day.

After we moved away, we'd all talk with her on the phone on Saturday nights while we watched *Hee Haw* or *The Lawrence Welk Show* with the sound down low so we could hear her on the phone. "Grandma loves you," she'd say. "Don't tell your sisters, but you're my favorite."

I totally knew I was. But Grandma was kind and had told both my sisters that they were her favorites. We all believed her.

When I was older, she taught me to drive with both feet just like she did.

When I was older still, I wrote a coming out letter to my grandparents. I wanted to tell them who I was. She wrote back. A sweet, loving letter. But the best part was the outside where she wrote, "We love you. We love you. We love you." in tiny letters along the edges of both sides of the envelope. She'd ensured I wouldn't have to be nervous to open it. Bless her.

When she learned of my trip to Europe, she asked me to bring her some salt and pepper shakers. I didn't. I kept forgetting, and then when I found some, they were made of glass, and I was afraid to carry them home. I regret that so much. Such a small request, months before she died, and I selfishly disregarded it. It would've taken so little to make her so happy. To add to her salt and pepper shaker collection, the one she kept in a lighted rotating display case in the living room. I suck.

I hope she knew I loved her as much as she loved me.

* * *

The spring rains came to Salzburg heavy, hard, and fast. My feet were soggy and cold all day. I didn't actually mind, though. I wore an excellent pair of Merrell lace-ups, water resistant, cushioned, good tread. I thought of them as hiking shoes, but they were just high-quality walking shoes. In Salzburg, with the exception of going to the opera house in Tevas and thick socks, I wore the Merrells.

Here's a tip. Do not order Mexican food in Austria. Do not. What kind of idiot would ask themselves, "I wonder what Austrians think tacos taste like??" IDIOT. Get hooked on potato soup instead, it warms your soul and your feet. Better than hot coffee on a Seattle ferry. Better than tacos in Texas.

Most days in Salzburg I'd walk around all morning, go back to the hostel kitchen to make a simple lunch, then lie on my bunk to rest and air out my socked feet for a little while. Salzburg's air was heavy and cool and damp.

The cold seeped into the floors first, then the walls, then your blood, and finally your bones where it overstayed its welcome. Just like in Seattle. No wonder I loved living there years later. Light wet snow, cold rain, swift rivers, the draw of hot heavy food and REI brand pullovers. Coffee. So much coffee. And classical music – KING FM.

One afternoon on my walk to yet another Sacher-Torte and cappuccino, it began to snow. Impossibly large, fluffy flakes. I was on a bridge, walking across the Salzach River as the snow fell on my nose and eyelashes. A delicious moment. My heart sang. I opened my umbrella to keep the wetness off my neck.

Salzburg had flowers too, lots of flowers I'd never seen before. Green grass, snowy peaks, hills covered in tall quiet trees. Salzburg was a premonition. A foreshadowing. A delight.

The dorm was clean and bright, four sets of bunk beds – 8 girls to each room. The student residents were mostly gone for a long holiday. The rooms were without any personal belongings, the dorm beds were rented out to travelers when the students were away. We each had a wooden locker, perfect for storing my large pack, spare shoes, and rolled up blanket. There was a small kitchen open to all, with various pots and pans, and a fridge with drawers for each room. Nobody ever took my groceries.

Was it a school? A church? I never quite figured it out. There was a small cemetery on the back side of the property. A suspicious number of young men buried in the summer of 1669. What was happening then? A raid? A plague?

Among the residents who had stayed behind was an opera singer who didn't go home for the holidays. There were other music students who carried their cellos and violin cases down the stairs to the cobblestone streets to practice near the shops frequented by tourists, open cases or upturned hats on the ground, collecting some coins as they played. This made me wonder why U.S. students are locked up in carrels, reserved ahead of time, sometimes paying rent to use them. I get it for pianists or harpists, but still.

Also, why do U.S. buskers need permits? Money, that's why. Taking their money.

Mila tried to explain a few things to me one afternoon: "Americans are dirty. Why must you come to my country – THIS country, I'm Italian – why must you come here and leave your McDonald's wrappers on the beach? On the sidewalk? In the autobus? What is wrong with you? You have no respect!"

These weren't questions, but even if they were, I couldn't answer them. Joy, another student, looked sympathetic, watching from the far corner of the bench they both sat on. I faced them on a stool. I didn't know what to say other than deny being a litterbug myself. If we were outdoors, Mila would've spat at that.

"And," she added, "you are not honest. None of you are honest with me, with the police, with yourselves. No honesty."

She had a point. I had only stopped tossing cigarettes out the car window recently when a friend freaked out, seeing me do it on a trip through a wooded area. Deer eat butts. I hadn't known. I hadn't learned anything yet about protecting the environment. I grew up in a church family that didn't believe men could damage God's grand creation, the populated earth. To this day, 25 years later as I write this, they deny global warming and climate change. Man's not powerful enough, they say.

I have long seen Earth as a wet dog, shaking off fleas. She violently shakes herself left and right and left again, to rid herself of these fleas, the human pests. Earthquakes, tsunamis, heat waves, food insecurity, disease. The wet dog is going to get rid of us all eventually.

Joy's lips were pursed, but she remained silent. Crocheting, taking a break from her vocal exercises. She too is a singer. She will have finals soon. I get it. I was a music major once; a bad one, but still, I know what they're asked to do. Crocheting would've been a good idea for me too probably.

Mila seemed to want an answer. She was demanding I speak for my "countrymen." All I could think of was America is a teenager. I must've read that somewhere. We're too young, as a country, to be wise. We're spoiled brats. Was it Franklin? Payne? I don't know who to quote.

During my hesitation, she snorted. Said, "you don't know either."

No, I don't. I can't speak for every rude bastard.

This was my first grilling as an American abroad. There would be more on this trip, and the next, and other times when talking with foreign residents visiting the U.S. – colleagues and neighbors. They all want to know when we're going to be better citizens. They all want to know why we suck when we have so much.

Mila was angry, but I didn't yet understand that her anger was fully justified. It absolutely was. Even more so today. Sometimes I have wanted the global community to teach us a lesson or two, to show us how to be respectful and appropriate and fair. But we have too much money, too much power. Too much land. Too much tangled up in other economies. Just too much.

I had shopped in a local grocery store for my lunch ingredients. There were surprisingly few options. Milk - two kinds. Bread, just a couple. Packaged cookies – the question was yes or no, not what kind. Things are probably different now, perhaps largely in part due to us. As I edit this years later, I find myself thinking of Thomas Friedman, though *The World is Flat* was 8 years away still.

Joy asked what I was doing Friday night. I had no plans, just exploring, wandering, whatever. She knew I didn't usually stay out late.

"My friend can't go to a musical with me. I have an extra ticket. You should come."

Mila got up and left, huffy.

We went to see *West Side Story* in German. GERMAN! She worried I wouldn't enjoy it, not speaking German – but no way. I knew the story. It would be fine. How special to see it produced in another country, in such a magical locale. Joy assuaged my panic about clothing. Told me to just wear whatever I had, which was a black sleeveless jumper dress with small white flowers, Tevas, thick hiking socks for the walk back after dark (hey, the color scheme worked). My green Polartec pullover. The one I slept in when I got too cold.

Joy laughed a friendly laugh when she saw me, and off we went.

It was already dark outside. Everyone on the street as we approached the theater – was it the Grosses Festspielhaus? The Salzburger Festspiele? I didn't know. I just thought of it as the opera house that used to be a horse stable, built into the rock at the base of one of Salzburg's 3 mountains, the Mönchsberg. Everyone else was wearing long dress coats and grown-up evening attire. Not me, the ridiculous American. But then I had to ask myself how many guests were actually living out of backpacks? Hmm. Who cares what others think?

The building was amazing. Outside you could see that it once served as a horse's stable, each of the five brass doors are curved at the top, like the places in the cemetery (what's it called, what are the "places" called? Open tombs?) where a family could hide from soldiers before running off?

Each door was engraved. Joy interpreted for me before we entered, "The Muse's holy house is open to those moved by song / god lifts those who are inspired… or, close enough," she said. Close enough. Beautiful design, I felt rich just looking at the sumptuous décor, being surrounded by it like a little cocoon of luxury in a place that, well, had seen its share of passion and magic – the Salzburg Festival happens here, and this hall has heard everything from Strauss to Mozart to Haydn, all the greats.

I caused quite a stir in the ladies' room. You haven't seen disapproval until you've rubbed elbows with the rich and powerful in Austria while wearing Texas beach clothes in a sold-out historical venue. Some of the dresses those women were wearing cost more than my annual salary for the next ten years. Twenty maybe. I don't know, I'm pretty clueless. But the jewelry made me wonder – do those necklaces live in black velvety boxes inside a safe behind a gilt-framed family painting in one of those two story royalty-painted houses with columns announcing the entrance? And their rings. Wow, the rings. I will never have that kind of money, I know. But I also hope I never give others that kind of disapproving look. (Spoiler alert – I sure as hell will, just not as stately, nor as well-heeled. And I never cluck, no matter how old I get.)

Upturned noses couldn't wipe the grin off my face. No matter what they thought of me, I was *there*. In that place, at that time, with two thousand other ticket holders. An unlikely visitor, but a happy one.

We sat upstairs to the left of the widest stage I'd ever seen. The curtains rose to polite applause, and there it was. *West Side Story*. Although, Mr. Shakespeare, the narrator who looked a bit like Beetlejuice, or Einstein, or their love child, was entirely unexpected. The role of Mr. Shakespeare was, fittingly, portrayed by a woman. Mr. Shakespeare periodically inserted himself into the scene and pleaded with the gangs on stage to stop their fighting, stop the madness, a tragedy is about to occur! And he was the matchmaker who ensured Tony and Maria's privacy so they could develop their love story in the correct scene.

Mr. Shakespeare was a nice touch, particularly when he (she!) sang "Somewhere" with such longing. Tony and Maria both had lovely singing voices as well. Tony's voice was just heavenly. I didn't want the songs to end, didn't want a return to dialogue.

Speaking of dialogue, the cursing was in English. The dancers chanted about being Jets in English, but certain terms were in Spanish "vamos" and "en tu familia" (see Antwerp bitches! See?). Everything else was in German. What a treat this evening was, what a gift this kind music student had passed on to me.

On the way back, she implored me to stay "present in the arts," to keep enjoying museums and music, plays and musicals and symphonies, paintings and outdoor sculpture and architecture and whatever else I could embellish my life with. Embellish my life. Yes. Thank you, Joy.

We walked across the Salzach River in comfortable silence, when a group of rowdy college boys approached, and began whistling at and catcalling not her (she was pretty hot) but me, until finally one of them burst out laughing, "Do you play football? Or soccer?" And they moved on, dancing around each other laughing and chugging a beer they passed between them.

They were making fun of my masculine frame, my muscled calves and broad shoulders, and it hurt. It did. Fuckers. I'll always remember that unnecessary jab, that transient cruelty. How harassing me and pointing out my differentness made them appear more normal to one another. I hope their future sons aren't standing outside libraries protesting drag queen story hour somewhere as I type this 25 years later. Assholes.

The next day while journaling about the events of the last evening, I enjoyed another afternoon dessert: a white and chocolate cake covered in a thick pink icing with a cherry on top. Punschtorte. I liked it even better than Sacher-Torte, and wouldn't have another piece until 2019 at a coffee shop in Sunnyvale, California.

OMG if I hear "Chattanooga Choo Choo" one more time…

Café Winkler, atop Mönchsberg (Monk's Hill). I went there for the view, which is incredible. It's high up on a cliff, overlooking Old Town and the river and in the distance there are other hills and even some Alps I think. Some guy yesterday tried to talk me into going with him and his friends to Innsbruck to ski. I've never skied and don't have any idea how that would impact the rest of my trip

– especially my budget – so I declined but will always wonder if I should have accepted. Travel, there should be some spontaneity to it, yes?

Anyway, the café. I sat there writing in my journal trying to figure out how to be a novelist. I was writing god-awful text that I don't plan to share with anyone ever. Except Nick, a friend back in Austin, who joined me a few weeks later at Little City Coffee on Congress Ave. He helped me see a few sentences that stood out. I've circled them in red, the possible keepers in my attempt to learn to write.

Café Winkler was next to the casino, and lunch wasn't cheap. I didn't spend $50 for lunch, but I did have a cappuccino (while looking across town at Kapuzinerberg!) and a disappointingly dry slice of Sacher-Torte. I made a salad later back at St. Sebastian.

Salzburg loves tulips and roses.

I walked all three "hills" in Salzburg. Mönchsberg, Festungsberg, and Kapuzinerberg.

High atop Kapuzinerberg is the small and sparse Capuchin monastery. The monks – or are they friars? – have always worn brownish robes, coffee-colored robes. I don't believe I saw any that day, but the building was beautiful for its simplicity. The chapel was hushed and invited contemplation, and of course the view of Salzburg and the surrounding mountains was stunning. I stayed as long as I could.

I found a small bar near my hostel and went to it every night between dinner and bed. It was a quiet place, with a friendly proprietor, big wooden tables, dart boards. I would order a soda and nurse it all night. The friendly proprietor didn't speak English, but I pointed to things and he brought them to me. We tried everything. German? No. French? No. I had discovered back in Paris that waiters sometimes speak up to 7 languages, but here this really nice guy and I couldn't find any language in common. That's my fault. I pretty much just speak English. But he let me write there. We played hangman with pen and paper. And he left me alone as long as I wanted. A nice, quiet place to write.

I didn't figure out how to write a novel during those evenings at the bar, but I did enjoy my six weeks with no job and a lot of blank pages. I still have the pen I used. It's got a few scrapes and dents, but it's also got this history in it. It was there, everywhere I went. And when it stopped writing years later, I set it aside, put it in my safekeeping box with other trinkets and old tickets and rocks and coins and photos, until finally I tried to fix it. And voila! It is restored and sitting next to this laptop. The tools have changed so much.

One night I dreamt of Georg, the father in *The Sound of Music*. He was in a field much like my grandfather's, dark soil, row upon row upon row of young green plants rising above the earth that nurtured them. Georg wore his usual gray dress slacks and shiny black shoes. Short sleeved white button up, casual like he was on a patio in the afternoon pouring lemonade into children's cups – leisurely. Not a hair out of place as he held up a recently plucked bunch of spinach.

The image was stylized. All the colors were washed out, reminding me of the postcards of the 70's, and each row of vegetables was labeled in typed rectangular cutouts pasted onto the postcard above the row in the field, "Spinach" "kale" "parsley." Snapshot-still, he smiled and looked directly at me. Blinked.

Later that day, I found myself sitting and smoking with another girl who lived at St. Sebastian full time. She was a painter from Italy, studying communications. A friend of hers, a German guy, joined us and they talked about art and Italian politics and the fact that Wolf Dietrich came from the Medici family, so much of the architecture in Salzburg was Italian. We made coffee and talked. A Russian girl, Katie, joined us and modeled her costume and makeup for a concert (opera) she was going to be in on Sunday. We teased her that the silly skirt she had to wear was sexy, and then we all tried to sing opera. The Italian showed me pictures of her paintings. Then we had a fun conversation about languages. They'd point to an object, then say the word in German, then English, then Italian. I added a few Spanish words. Like this:

Zigaretten, cigarette, cigarillo

Zucker, sugar, sucar, azucar

Kafee, café, coffee, café

Milk, milk, leche, leche

An older Austrian woman joined us. She worked for MIT for 10 years. We discussed Catholicism, Prussia, Clinton's education proposals, Peru, Austrian history, Wolf Dietrich again. She too found the crucifix to be cruel. Politics, economics, literature. Tolstoy and Dostoevsky and Gabriel Garcia-Marquez, Collette and Goethe. She said that on September 15th, the Italians may decide to split north and south Italy, mostly because northern Italians felt like they were having to support southern Italy. So, as always, taxes were the issue.

I felt lucky to be learning and promised myself I'd keep doing it. Always.

She told me that if I stayed in Austria, they'd put me through grad school. Free. The Austrian government invested in people, believing that an educated populace would inevitably lead to public good. She asked if I'd like to stay.

Hell yes, I would. But I was afraid. Too afraid.

I jotted all this down in my journal at Pepe Gonzales's Tapas Bar, where the salsa sucked hard. (I learned later that grad school wasn't actually free for Americans, but it was incredibly cheap compared to the U.S.)

My ankle was hurting again. Too many hills, but worth it.

About a week into my stay, I set off to see Nonnberg Abbey. I walked the winding path along the stone wall to the top of the hill where you could see all the city, all the hills, all the churches below. Salzburg is such a beautiful place.

The abbey wasn't open to the public, but the cemetery below, Salzburg's oldest – St. Peter's cemetery was. It was an important hiding place in *The Sound of Music.* Haydn's brother is buried here, and Mozart's sister Anna. She is buried near the entrance, the ancient catacombs carved into the rock overhead.

The tour of the catacombs cost a whopping 80 cents. I think. Money conversion isn't my forte.

The catacombs were made out of natural caves created by conglomerate rock formations in the Ice Age. As early as 2500 BC, Roman Christians entered the caves from the secret tunnel that began near where the cable car is today. There also used to be a Roman castle where the medieval Hohensalzburg fortress is now.

The woman giving the tour told us that on July 16, 1669, there was a landslide that killed 220 people. The cross-shaped chapel built close to the top of the mountain was split in half, lengthwise. Half a cross. The rest rained down on the town below. Shops, churches, houses, a seminary (so that's why there are so many young men's graves from that date!) were all destroyed. She told us that there have been no more rockslides since the Felsputzers started coming every year.

I raised my hand. "What is a Felsputzer?" She didn't really know how to explain. She had a script in various languages, but she didn't have strong English skills.

I had to know more.

So, I had a question and a lot of time and nowhere in particular to be for close to a week. It was the makings of an adventure, a quest. What are the Felsputzers? What do they do? Who are they?

I started at a small indie bookstore I'd discovered a few days before, on Bergstrasse, near Bosna café. I wish I could remember the name, and the name of the delightful bookkeeper who ran it. A kind gentleman who had explained to me a few days before that Maria Von Trapp had written her own book, one the tourists never asked for. So of course, I bought it from him. Now I was a patron. A real customer who could come to him on a mission – what's a Felsputzer?

He considered my question. Then said the only paragraph he could think of that used the term Felsputzer was in Diana Burgwyn's *Salzburg, A Portrait,* but the book was out of print. He told me that "Fels-Putzer" means mountain cleaning or mountain polishing. Then he told me Felsputzers are hired by the City. He jotted it down, tore off a small notepad page for me:

FELS-PUTZER. Hr. R_____.

Burgwyn: *Salzburg, a Portrait.*

And he drew a chisel.

I thanked him and went to Schloss-Mirabell to the government office. A clerk told me in his limited English that there wasn't any information he could share. No job description in English. He suggested if I really wanted to know more, I could apply for the job. So I did. He set up an immediate appointment for me with Herr

R_____ who took my paper application in hand and held the door to his small office for me.

He sat and stared at me, read the application, stared at me again.

"No," he said.

I feigned exasperation. "No? I would like to know more about the job."

"No. No no, it isn't done." He twisted his handlebar mustache while looking down at the paper again, flipping it over, looking back at me with searing blue eyes. "No. You are not strong."

Bastard! How does he know? (He was right, though I did take a weightlifting class the year before from an Olympic weightlifting coach, and I was the only girl they'd ever had in class who could do three sets of body dips using my full body weight.) Still.

"You must be a man." He squirmed as he said it to the American woman sitting in front of him.

Ah, now I get it. He was very uncomfortable, worried about what I would say or do next. I decided to reassure him and told him I just wanted to understand. I wanted to be a writer. Actually, I embellished a bit. In the spirit of the adventure, I told him I was a novelist who was considering making one of my characters a Felsputzer but that I needed more information.

He smiled politely, but I could tell I was wasting his time. He quickly explained that Felsputzers are strong young men with broad backs and strong arms who can repel themselves up and down mountains very easily all day, safely, over and over. They remove loose rock and fill cracks with cement to keep the water out, to stabilize them. A successful candidate will need to be trained in building houses, stone by stone. It's hard, dangerous work, well-paid at about 50,000 shillings per month (60K/year USD). From November to February, they cut trees. They retire pretty quickly, changing careers once they marry.

There. Mission accomplished. What a nice man you are, Herr R_____. Thank you for the memory – the time I applied for a job in Salzburg.

The next night I met a woman named Suzie at the hostel. Her name made me think of John Irving's Susie the Bear. Suzie was Austrian and wanted to live in Salzburg. She said she didn't think it was too boring like others did. We talked about sex and love and Americans and Europeans and racism.

It was great. Strangers are free to say so much to one another, knowing the words are fleeting. She quoted an Italian poet whose loosely translated words I managed to approximately scribble down:

*Love enters the eyes and goes to the heart. The pain
of love begins in the heart and goes out through
the eyes – in the form of tears.*

Was she interpreting and quoting Petrarch? Thanks to the Internet, I suspect so.

That last night in Salzburg, I went back to the bar to write. I bade the friendly proprietor goodbye in Spanish without even thinking, "Adios!" and he laughingly responded, "Viajes secures, mi amiga!"

Seven days and it didn't occur to either of us to try Spanish. But we laughed heartily about it that night.

I bought John Irving's *Son of the Circus* on my way to the train station the next morning. Would there be a dancing bear in this one? I'd have bet good money there would be.

It was time to go. So long, Austria. So long.

The train wended its way through mountain passes, up the sides of great gray mountains with green valleys below dotted by picturesque little villages. Wispy smoke rose from tiny chimneys, I could almost smell the fireplaces. Like model train sets, towns come to life. Quiet, pastoral, picturesque life.

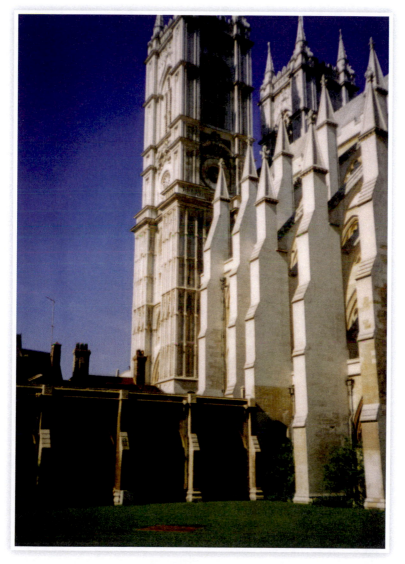

London Westminster Abbey

Notre Dame's flying buttresses before the fire

Outside the Louvre

Salzburg St. Peter's Cemetery

Salzburg Salzach River

Rome Colosseum

Florence Duomo with Baptistery shadow

Red
roofs in
Finale
Ligure

Cliffs
meet
ocean in
Finale
Ligure

Espresso
on the
beach in
Finale
Ligure

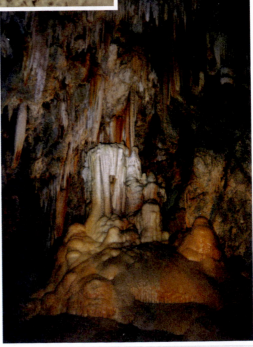

Liguria
caves

Greenpeace ship in Monaco

Nice Promenade des Anglais

Venice

I fucking hated Venice.

First, I was looking for Vaporetto 82 (now known as Vaporetto Number 2) without understanding why that word starts with "vapor" and so I kept wandering around looking for streets with bus stops, but I couldn't find any.

Let me just say that again. I kept looking for the streets, but I couldn't find any.

I'd like to reiterate here. I had known there were canals, and buildings growing out of the water, but I did not know that you couldn't find a *street* from the train station.

I walked and walked – I don't know where I was walking if I wasn't on a street, but I wasn't. Were they alleys? I don't know.

Bridges by and around and over water, yes. No real streets. My feet hurt. My ankle burned and throbbed. I was hot and I wanted to sit and to eat and to figure out where the hell my hostel was before dark so I could sleep indoors this night. Could I not just find a cool bottle of water somewhere? No, I could not.

Eventually I saw it, a small foot ferry with the number 82 on it. God damn I am slow sometimes.

The first ferry to start loading passengers was too full, so I had to wait for the next one. People pushed and shoved and rudely forced my body into the side of the boat like I was doing something wrong. I was, actually. I didn't know it until years later, when I read online that the locals absolutely hate it when tourists take the commute time ferries wearing huge 50 lb. packs, which is exactly what I had done.

People kept pushing and shoving the whole 30-minute trip to San Marco Square. Which wasn't my destination, no. That particular #82 didn't stop at my stop, it skipped it. So I had to buy another ticket, queue up again, and take another foot ferry – this time with a man's shoulder and underarm in my face the whole way.

(Twenty years in the future, riding the commuter buses away from Seattle's up and coming South Lake Union at the end of the day, I'd have to stand again with my face in men's underarms as they held onto the overhead rail to keep from falling as we careened down the road, standing, smashed together like sardines. The vaporetto was training, I guess, though I never did get used to it. Hated it every time, every place.)

I did eventually find the hostel. It was on an island made of concrete, no businesses nearby. No food, no restaurant for dinner. And of course, being a concrete island, I couldn't just keep walking until I found a place. I walked anyway. What else could I do? The place was a deserted, filthy concrete island. The canal was filthy and smelled. The hostel did serve dinner, thank goodness.

The hostel was pretty much a large warehouse full of beds – one single room full of rowdy young people who couldn't settle down. Hundreds of them. I imagined this is what emergency shelters look like when you're evacuated from a hurricane zone in Miami or something. Rows upon rows of beds, you can see everyone. And there was nowhere to lock my pack. I slept with my money belt on, kept my daypack zipped onto my large pack, and used it to snuggle up to as if I were in bed with an unshapely human. There were so many young people in that hostel that night. Laughing, talking, drinking, dancing. I got little sleep and decided I had seen enough.

The ferry ride back to the train station the next morning was nice though. The boat had to go out into the sea a tiny bit to avoid other boats. It was a nice quiet early morning ride with a pastel sky starting to light up the day. At the train station there was a wait for my train to Rome, so I sat outside on the concrete steps which were dotted with other backpackers.

There was one girl in particular I remember, by herself, with a pack like mine, sitting reading. I sat near her. Near enough that she looked up and said hello and we chatted to kill the time. Where are you from, where are you going, where have you been (why am I thinking of Joyce Carol Oates?) and how long. The usual. Plus, because there was time, a little of the "who are you" conversation. She had sewn a patch of the Canadian flag – red and white, with the maple leaf in the center – onto her navy backpack in a prominent spot near the top. I wondered, who does that? Who sews their country's flag onto their backpack? That must be a lot of pride. Something I just couldn't relate to.

Eventually, as the conversation petered out, I asked why she had the flag on her backpack. Why so prominently? Her answer was simple. "So, people don't mistake me for one of you."

Holy fuck.

Rome

"I was smart. I just had a thick layer of stupid
that had settled on top of me."

Kevin Wilson, *Nothing to See Here*

My next journal entry simply says, "I came to Rome this
morning." I'll admit that I had been looking forward to the
long train ride through Italy. Like in that movie Meg Ryan was in,
French Kiss, all the beautiful countryside. I was ready to sit and watch
a beautiful Italy roll by. Wineries in particular. But no. It was early
April. Nothing but dirt and empty fields. All the vines I saw were
stripped.

But it was a good long rest, that train ride.

I had called ahead to reserve a bed in a small hostel in the middle of Rome. I arrived at 5pm local time, knew what train station I needed to get to in order to walk to it, but I couldn't find that train station on any of the maps on the walls. How do you arrive at a train station that isn't on the map? Clearly, I was at fault.

Locals know the places they live, so I went to the Metro ticket window to ask the man working and living here, "How do I get to…" and pointed to my destination on the map in my *Let's Go Europe* book. I don't speak any Italian at all. But I was pointing to my destination and asked "how."

He took my money, gave me a ticket, pointed to the ceiling, and said "up."

OK, got it. On the wall maps, north is always up. So I must go north.

I hopped a northbound train and two stops later I figured it out. I had been AT my destination when he sold me that ticket. "Up" meant literally, go up the stairs, outside, you're here. Up.

And I didn't have to buy that ticket after all. God damnit, as my friend Tara would say in her pure Texas drawl. Gawd dammmmiiiIIiiiit.

I walked back, which took a while, then found my hostel, and went out again to find some dinner. Unlike Venice, Rome has lots of streets. Lots and lots. Food too, sometimes sold right on the streets.

Italians are loud. Their language is percussive with its shouts and stories and cadence and laughter.

Not far from the train station I saw two drag queens, dressed really nice in heels and miniskirts – not flamboyant – and realized I had a chance to ask for information that did not exist in my *Let's Go Europe* book. Where do I find and meet girls? Specifically, where's the lesbian bar?

They would know, right?

I started thinking of Spanish words that might work. I landed on "discotec" – a dance hall, or club maybe? (Wrong!) They didn't speak any English, but they hooked elbows with me and we started prancing gayly down a cobblestone alley, going… somewhere. A gay bar perhaps.

That's when it hit me. They weren't dressed flamboyantly, they weren't larger than life. They weren't going to a drag show. They had stiletto heels and tiny purses and bright pink lipstick. I had picked up 2 transvestite hookers! (My editor wife would like to insert that yes, I know this is inappropriate language *now*, but it was the only language I had back *then*.)

Finally in a quiet spot, the taller one with better English stopped and asked if I smoke. Sure, and I held up my pack of Galouses to offer her one. No, no. Then they used hand signals to ask something about needles in the arm. Dang – shooting up? What the hell were they asking me? One of them stuck out her tongue, grabbed it with her hand, and said "A-CHID." Pinching and rubbing her tongue.

Acid?

They were pleased. Yes, ACHID.

No, no no. I do not have ACHID.

"American?" she asked.

See, if I'd had a Canadian flag on my day pack, they wouldn't have asked me that.

I was trying to figure out how to extricate myself from this situation when we turned a corner. I fell off the curb and landed on my hands and knees in the street. The pretty one picked me up and took my arm. A cop started down the alley toward us. They ran, I did not. The cop said, "Go back to the hostel, American."

And that's exactly what I did. There was a group about to go to dinner, so I joined them. Safety in numbers.

It was a lavish, overpriced dinner with a loud group of American college students who had more money than sense. We passed a throng of people trying to see some French movie starlet in a tiny little hole in the wall with excellent wine nearby. I managed to sneak off and back to the hostel to bed alone. No "discotec" for me. I didn't date all through college to avoid distractions. I knew I was likely to become obsessed again, like I did with straight girls I had crushes on.

I knew I was barely making it to and through all my classes working full time. I knew dating just hadn't been the goal. But now, here, on vacation in Europe? I'd keep looking for lesbian bars, if there was such a thing in Europe in 1997.

I went to the Vatican Museum, first walking through iconic St. Peter's Square. From the 1500's. I thought that was old. But give me ten minutes…

Indoors I saw a mummy of a woman with dyed hair, 2000 BC. We've always had standards of beauty, right? And women's fiery temperament was depicted in the Statue of Lion Goddess by Sekhmet, 1390 BC. Some things are universal, across time.

Laocoon and his sons! Was the sculpture really dated 50 B.C.? Did it really depict the events that led to the founding of Rome? What drama, what action, what history in a single statue. Man is amazing. (So is that snake). Talk about a masterpiece.

And the Sistine Chapel, *Touch of Adam*. How? Just how did Michaelangelo paint that in 1508? My neck was sore just looking at it briefly. Speaking of drama. I wish I had days to just stand here and stare. Of course I bought a postcard. A really long one.

And! *Achilles and Ajax Playing a Board Game* – it's not at the Louvre after all, no, it's here! I knew it from the doorway. Black on red, ancient Greek pottery, 530 BC. Look how engaged they are. Look how much detail is still there after all these years, how pristine it is. The color, the action and concentration depicted. They are both moving and not. The jar's handles have hearts, rows of hearts, the top row upside down and the bottom row right side up so that the curves almost touch. I drew them in my journal, though how accurately I drew them is questionable.

The Vatican museum was full of beauty, as you'd expect. But also crowded and hard to move around in.

Afterwards, I headed for the Pantheon and the Column of Trajan, and finally the Colosseum. The Pantheon is an architectural marvel. First a Roman temple, now a Catholic church. It's just astounding to stand inside this place. Also, how did all that weight of the dome stay up all these years, without support beams? Sometimes I swear modern tools make us dumber than we used to be.

Afterward, I found a small café across the Piazza della Rotonda and people watched until I was rested enough to head toward the Colosseum.

It started to rain as soon as I arrived. The tourists poured out, a steady stream of colorful umbrellas. I looked at the Arch of Constantine across the street. And then I realized I could go into the Colosseum when it was less crowded – they hadn't closed it, so I went in. The few of us who did go in had unobstructed views, which would not have been possible just a few minutes before.

Snap snap snap. Photos with more raindrops than people in them. Me with a wet flannel overshirt and drooping bangs. Fogged up glasses. But the rain stopped then, as quickly as it had begun. I stood there, seeing it all. Imagining the bloody battles, the victories, the defeats. Crowds cheering. Death and watching death and cheering death. Football without the ball.

What a roar! Were there echoes in an open-walled place like this? There were surely echoes over time, ripples in the fabric that ties then and now together. History.

I did Rome in a day, I really did. Well, I missed out on DaVinci, but otherwise, I saw quite a lot.

The next day I went back, to the Forum, and sat on the foundation of an old ruin of a building – I know today that my American was showing. Stupid and thoughtless and curious without even knowing – ignorance – that my Levi's didn't belong on that rock. Should never have touched it. And yet, I've never forgotten it. I sat there with my pen and journal. I liked it there. The Colosseum was off to my right somewhere, Piazza Venezia to my left. Trajan's Forum across the street, in front and to my left. But here, the ruins are down, below the city and its modern cacophony. It's protected from the roar of the city.

With each step I took, I heard echoes of ancient soldiers' footfalls on the rocky soil. Crunch, crunch. It must have been so beautiful here. It still is.

The sky was clear. What a beautiful day. Hot sun, cool shade. I wandered into Villa Borghese gardens. It was a gorgeous Sunday and people were out strolling. The musical trio called Tarahumara had been playing. Pan pipe, a tiny guitar, cello. So beautiful and I sat in the shade under the trees, high above and overlooking this eternal city.

I took a few notes, but otherwise didn't write – just enjoyed my time there.

Later that afternoon I was outside on a bench, near the hostel, reading my travel guide to figure out if there were any museums or other things nearby that I could go see with my free afternoon. I was smoking under a tree, people watching, when a young man approached and asked if he could sit on the bench with me. Then he introduced himself and asked if it would be ok to practice speaking English with me. Absolutely. That's the kind of interaction that makes travel what it is. You never know what you'll learn. Or if you'll end up with tickets to *West Side Story*.

Mauricio was young and cute but not in a way that the young girls probably appreciated. Eager, dorky, definitely from Rome. He knew a lot about it. He charmed me into going for gelato at "the best place" that shouldn't be missed and wouldn't be in any guidebooks.

Have I mentioned how much gelato I'd eaten in just two days? Like with Sacher-Torte, I had been testing out various versions of the dessert. They serve it in three small scoops, so you get three flavors in your little cup. A little pink plastic spoon. I think I always got stracciatella, vanilla with chocolate shavings. I resisted fruit and pistachio flavors. Chocolates and coffees are my favorites. Since then, I've come to know that the best gelato isn't chocolate. Limone, fregola, noce di cocco. I didn't know what these words meant, so I avoided them. Terrible error of judgment.

Mauricio pointed out that "the best place" was right around the corner. Why not? We were in a pretty open area with lots of foot traffic, sure. I'm not afraid of everyone, just bad guys. Mauricio was too little and too dorky to be a bad guy. And my money and passport were tucked safely away in my money belt. Sure.

We went somewhere. I don't remember, but we had gelato, and it was good. Very creamy. He convinced me to try the pistachio, which is my favorite now. He'd been telling me about his brother, his super cool brother, the bowling star (that's a thing?) when suddenly, oh! Imagine that! Here we were at the front door of the bowling alley. Let's go meet him!

Mauricio practically begged. He never got to talk to girls, please come meet his brother so he could have some honor.

Oh my god, okay.

We went in. It was a small, dark bowling alley, quieter than those I'd visited at home. No fluorescent lights overhead, no loud music. It was the kind of place where people practiced, and sure enough, there was Mauricio's tall, lanky, gorgeous, olive-skinned brother with his perfect hair and his perfect chest and his sexy, open, vertically striped bowling jersey and the rolled-up sleeves showing off his manicured biceps and forearms.

I felt a little sorry for the dork, growing up in that shadow, trying to become a young man under that suave perfect Italian hunk's shadow. The women must flock around this older brother. Actually, he did have an entourage. They were sitting quietly batting their eyelashes so he could concentrate. He wasn't thrilled to be interrupted to meet me, but his eyes showed a little playful understanding.

We didn't stay long. Just long enough for me to stare at those muscles and Mauricio to get nervous that he was letting his brother outshine him for no reason, so we went back outside to talk and smoke. Eventually, he offered to give me a tour. The kind of tour only the locals can give.

I got in his car.

Stupid.

I got in his car.

Or someone's car whose keys he was able to get off his brother before we left the bowling alley. Probably it was his brother's. But he knew the car, knew where it was parked, how it handled. We hopped in. I was pretty excited really, getting to see the city without a bus and with his explanations, not the canned tourist guide's explanations.

"We call this the typewriter" he said as we whizzed along Piazza Venezia square, past the wedding cake shaped edifice, white with so many columns I couldn't count them, sitting atop a hill, beckoning entry. It was lovely. I thought he said it was a city building, like a courthouse or something, but it is a museum and monument called

Altare della Patria (Altar of the Fatherland). Breathtaking, so much artistry in a building. All I could think of was *Roman Holiday*, and that this was mine. We didn't have a scooter, but the little car sounded and felt like it had a scooter engine under its hood and that's as close as I was going to get.

It was thrilling and terrifying all at once, the speed with which he drove, staying in the flow of traffic, around all the other cars in the traffic circles, right up to and past any pedestrians crossing the road – and that is why I had such a hard time crossing the road in Rome. I was scared to do it really. The cars, they just expect you to keep moving and they will go around you without stopping or slowing and it is terrifying. I spent a ton of time walking away from traffic circles rather than through them, because the very idea was just too terrifying. The locals did it, and other tourists. The cars whizzed past. Nope. Not me.

Mauricio drove and drove, happily, confidently, showing me his city.

Then things got weird. He wanted to kiss at stoplights. He was driving one-handed, stroking the back of my neck with his right. I tried to scoot out of reach, but the car was small, and his arms were long. He started protesting, talking about love, talking about ... who knows. I couldn't hear a thing after he licked his finger and stuck it in my ear, like that was supposed to turn me on – news flash! Not sexy, guys, especially not when the girl is already saying no. I said no over and over. He protested, thought it was some sort of game, that I was being coy. I asked him to stop the car. Told him to. Stop the car.

And it hit me with a sick stomach feeling, a thud, a drop, a nauseating realization – I was in the middle of a foreign country, in a large city, in a strange man's car, lost, going who knows where, and I had no way out.

Nobody in the entire world knew where I was.

If he didn't let me out of the car, I was going to be in trouble.

He was laughing, enjoying his romantic afternoon with The American. He would remember this for a long time. Or did he do it all the time and I had underestimated him? Maybe he was in the habit of picking up girls. Who knows? He wouldn't stop. I begged. I said no a lot. I told him I was a lesbian.

He laughed so hard I was afraid he would wreck the car.

"I've heard that one before."

Oh dear, I was really in trouble. I pulled out all the stops with, "My mama. She cries and cries I am lesbian." And hung my head.

Those were the magic words. I had brought mama into the equation. He quickly pulled over near a Metro stop, kicked me out, and sped off.

Go back to the hostel, American.

It was stories like this one that inspired my wife (pronouns: they/them) to start saying I am a Darwin Award waiting to happen. Or that I should have been a Darwin Award. Or that I'm lucky I wasn't a Darwin Award winner. There are various iterations, but all represent sheer disbelief that I'm still alive and in one piece. And they try to forbid me from talking to strangers, especially at bus stops. They think it's ok to talk to bartenders and street vendors at the farmer's market. Retail employees. But not random customers, not people sitting next to me on the bus, or walking around a beach with a camera, or the guy with three tripods shooting the Space Needle and Mt. Rainier from Kerry Park in Queen Anne or sitting outside a coffee shop on Congress Avenue in Austin. The guy ordering breakfast tacos right behind me. Randos.

I can't help myself.

Randos make the world go round.

Florence

The next day I headed to Florence without any idea it was free museum day. O.M.G. So many children!

Had a marvelous lunch of pasta, roast beef, peas, fruit. For dinner I would have a slice of eggplant pizza. I ended up in a pretty, clean little pensione that had a balcony over a pretty little courtyard garden. So much green, fragrant green. I had roommates, and we sat outside talking for hours. The beds had sheets, and there was a luxurious shower in the room with my own little bar of soap. It was absolutely heaven to shower without using the Dr. Bronner's bottle in my bag.

In the morning I tried to find a place to stay another night in Florence, but no luck. I tried splurging on an actual hotel room, possibly sharing it with another lone traveler from Minnesota, but there was nothing we could afford. No hostels, no more rooms anywhere. Besides, the museums were so crowded with schoolchildren.

But I did stop by the Duomo – at least to see the engraved baptistry doors. As I stood there, really looking at them, trying to memorize them, these bronze reliefs from the mid 1400's, the *Gates of Paradise* as Michaelangelo called them, an acoustic guitar began strumming softly behind me. Everyone around me turned their heads as a young teen boy began to grunge-growl his way through "Smells Like Teen Spirit" with a thick Italian accent. He and a small group of pre-teen guitarists sat on the steps of the Duomo itself, a clutch of teen girls swooning as the boys did their best Nirvana impressions.

Why wasn't the smartphone invented yet? I really need that video, ya know?

With nowhere to stay, I headed north.

Hopped off the train in Pisa to see the famous leaning tower, which I could see from the train station. It was covered in scaffolding. It's also smaller than you'd think, and leaning more than you'd think. Fuck it. I came, I saw. Bought a souvenir replica in the gift shop and hopped right back on the very next northbound train. To the beach then.

Finale Ligure

The train ride was long and not terribly interesting at first. Hot and noisy, clackety clackety clack. So many people talking that it was easy to tune out the din. I let myself drift off, leaning my forehead against the window as I'd done on the way to Munich a few weeks before.

The flickering light woke me. Dark, light, dark, light.

My eyes opened to the most magnificent scene I had ever beheld. Shockingly blue Mediterranean waters. Cobalt blue under a pastel sky. Cousteau blue. A fathomless vast azure sea.

The train popped in and out of black empty tunnels and emerged again into the total opposite of black. The splendor knocked the wind right out of me before I was even fully conscious. We were high above the sea, hugging a rugged cliff. Rocks and small trees on the right, the endless Mediterranean on the left.

One of the best surprises of my life.

I have never slept on a train again, not once.

The train station was embedded in town, and from there I could only see shops and hills, but my guidebook included a crude map I followed to the Vuillermin Castle Hostel. So many stone steps up to the gate. My ankle protested. The rest of me ignored it.

The hostel was an old, repurposed castle high above the Mediterranean, above the beaches, above the town of Finale Ligure and its lovely red roofs dotting the slope down to the sea.

Each morning, I lingered over a strong morning coffee, sitting in the front courtyard near a knee-high stone wall, taking in the sheared cliffs and water and town. It was late spring, and there was just enough sun to warm my skin.

Breathing was easy.

I stayed about a week, walking down to town or the ocean each day, exploring churches, just sitting on the beach. While traveling off-season has its benefits, there are drawbacks, too. Closed restaurants and shops. No heat in the hostel. I kept sleeping in my pullover and a knit hat - a trick shared by a traveler from home.

Luckily, I did find an excellent Italian restaurant in the mostly closed cluster of small businesses catering to tourists near the water. The first time I stopped in, a lovely tall blonde waitress who looked an awful lot like my imaginary friend and fictional character, Claire, brought me a bowl of pasta. She explained that they were about to close for siesta and wouldn't open again until many hours later in the day. Later than I usually ate dinner. She said the restaurant would be lively and that dinners lasted for hours, with many courses. She also told me that Finale Ligure is a German resort town, and that the Germans weren't on holiday yet, so the locals had the run of the place. I should come down one night. I did, but it was so packed and so loud and so late, I chose instead to come back every afternoon before siesta and have a small plate of something to tide me over until I could find a reasonable dinner.

One day after my morning contemplation of the sea, I turned left after descending the steps and arrived once again at the water. My siren, the water. The ocean.

And I kept walking to the left, past town. Toward what looked like another castle atop a large rock outcropping. I never figured out what that building was, but noticed the road cut right through the rock below it, and there was a mini tunnel with a protected pedestrian path. I took it. How could I resist? Anything could be on the other side. Anything.

Of course, what I found there was more rock, more pristine sand, more blue ocean.

And a cave! I found a cave! A tiny little cave!

There were only four or five tourists on the chilly beach that day, but none in the cave. I plopped myself down right at the entrance in the only shade on the entire beach, mindful of dangers from inside the cave, as well as the tides.

I sat there for hours, alone, with only nature and a distant local beach walker in my view once the tourists left. What a tremendous gift, a moment of my own in this place. I hoped the mountain of rock overhead didn't give way.

I was sitting among tiny little rocks of many colors and shapes, even a pale red one with an almost yellow stripe. Time. I held the evidence of time in my hands. How did a dark gray rock with a thick white stripe get here? Or the green crystals embedded in a chalky white one, when the cliffs overhead and along the shore are almost tan in color? Light brown, with hints of red, depending on the light.

These little rocks had been smoothed by the ocean, my mistress, for how long? They surely started out jagged, not smooth and round. I appreciated the Time I was able to see and to touch; it's smooth cold surface solid in a way present time never is.

There were also seashells of course, and what I think is probably a jawbone, which I carried home in the safest vessel I had with me at the time – an empty Marlboro box. I still have that bone, and the lid of that box where I scrawled "Finale Ligure" so I would never forget where I found it.

I don't know why I carried a couple rocks and that bone around with me for twenty-five years, but I have done exactly that. I'd also like to take a moment here to acknowledge my ignorance and selfishness and eco-wrong behavior. Today I take photos instead. My own snapshots of Time.

Speaking of snapshots. 1997 was a whole different world. We had to use actual film and then have it developed at a store. After a few days, you could go pick up the physical prints. If you were lucky, you could get the photos from the film developers in under a week. They charged you more to do it quicker.

Also if you were flying with film, when you went through airport security, you had to take the film out of your carry on. I always took my rolls of film out of my checked luggage too, because the scanners could ruin the film entirely. So, you'd put the rolls of film in the big plastic security dish with your keys and pocket change. Yes, we still had pocket change then.

If you were lucky, you could afford double prints. It was the only way to actually share a photo (as opposed to showing one). If you were unlucky, some or all of those prints were out of focus or too dark or included your finger in the upper left corner.

By the time you knew a photo was a terrible fail, it was too late to do anything about it. The moment was lost forever, nothing to do but to grieve it.

Another problem - sometimes you ran out of film altogether before you ran out of things to photograph. Like me, on my last day in Finale Ligure, I asked a nice barista to take the last shot I had left – I wanted a picture of myself on the beach with a cappuccino, wearing my backpack and preparing to travel to my next stop. I'm so glad I did - it's one of my favorite photos of myself.

But goddamn if I wouldn't trade it for a shot of what I saw next – a tan, topless blond galloping her white horse along the water's edge, causing seabirds to scurry as she passed. She even waved at me.

God. Damn.

There was also a huge beautiful white swan just riding the waves.

But before that, back to the little cave where I watched a soft mist form over the water. Or was it spray from the small waves breaking in the afternoon breeze? Then mysteriously, a cloud dropped over the cliff above me and drifted down to the sand, draping a gauzy curtain between the cave and the rest of the world.

I swear, I'd just found Honah Lee! Alone, me and Honah Lee. Where is Puff? Oh Puff! Come out, come out wherever you are!

Grandma Polly had had a child's record player with brightly colored plastic records. We'd sit in her bedroom playing "Puff the Magic Dragon" and "(How Much Is) That Doggie in the Window?" while she did search-a-word puzzles and slathered her swollen feet in Corn Huskers. We all wanted a friend like Puff. We wouldn't outgrow him like Little Jackie Paper did.

An expensive top-down two-seater whizzed by on the highway above the beach carrying four young partiers laughing and singing. Reminded me of the time we stole – um, borrowed – a friend's dad's Mercedes convertible and flew down Dallas' 635 singing Tracy Chapman's "Fast Car," then Janis' "Mercedes Benz," and back to "Fast Car." Two of us sat high up on the close side of the trunk, feet dangling behind the car's two front seats as we held on to one another for dear life. Reckless fun.

In Finale Ligure, the icy cold water felt good on my ankle. The sand was really hard to walk on but felt so good when I buried my ankle in the sun-warmed grains.

The Pasqualini il Caffé was inland, small, moderately busy, but they didn't mind if I lingered. There were old men reading the papers, both alone and in groups. The young woman behind the counter was very nice. I wrote a lot.

The pizza joint I stopped in that night was blaring No Doubt's "Don't Speak." Better than Hasselhoff! A lot better! I ordered a thin wide slice, thinking that pepperoncini meant pepperoni. Ha! Nope!

Portishead. Yes. Thank you.

Once I'd had my fill of night beach, I headed back through town to the stone stairway leading up to the hostel. These weren't just any stairs. They were step-worn smooth, leading up and up to the top of the hill upon which the castle was perched. Many steps. Many many steps. With my ankle, I was lucky to be able to climb it each day.

The stairs led to a high wooden gate opening to the courtyard where I sipped my morning coffees. But this night, the gate was locked. I knocked. I knocked again. I pounded. Nothing. I yelled off and on, "Hello! The gate is locked! Hello!!" Again, nothing. Which was weird because just the day before a large group of middle schoolers had moved in. Even they were stone silent. And it was only 10:30pm.

The hostel manager lived on-site with his half-blind, fully deaf German shepherd. If I worked at it, maybe I could get the dog's attention anyway. She'd see the gate moving as I banged on it, or she'd sniff me while doing her rounds. But no, she heard and saw nothing. "Damn deaf dog! Useless watchdog!"

It was cold and getting colder. The prospect of going down all those steps, trying to find a phone somewhere to call the hostel – if they even answered at this hour – and climbing back up just seemed impossible. A risk probably not worth taking. Could I sleep up here on these stone steps? Probably not. The spiders would eat me. Maybe I'd end up sleeping on the beach. The cave was sort of protected, yes?

I kept hollering and banging until the hostel manager came running across the courtyard to unlock the door from inside, apologizing profusely. The kids were all tucked in with an early curfew, and everyone else was accounted for. He'd simply forgotten me.

Nobody in the entire world knew where I was. There are downsides to that, too.

One afternoon I shopped in a local store, just to have that experience. There was a small metal cream pitcher and two tiny little spoons that I couldn't resist. I have them still. I forgot to check for the salt and pepper shakers.

Eventually, a 40-ish lesbian moved into my room. She said she owned 50 acres in California and rented out cabins to women. They go around topless. She showed me a picture of them building a house topless. (P.S. my younger breasts were still pretty nice in comparison!) She rarely wears clothes. She doesn't watch movies or tv. Doesn't drink or smoke. No sugar or meat. Doesn't visit large cities, not even to see Europe! She plays mandolin. She camps, hikes, runs. She has no problem destroying big companies' logging equipment and feels guilty driving a car to town.

None of these things are bad. I think I like the idea of them all, so why am I so uncomfortable talking to her? I understand the problems with big cities. Maybe her life is richer than some, but it still felt sad to me. There's a separatism about it. I don't limit myself to women's spaces. I want straight friends and male friends, and to travel the world, to take pleasure in all the colors of the world. (Why were lesbian communes in the 90's always so white?? Are they still? I have no idea.)

One afternoon, I found myself on the beach near two other women who had chosen to sunbathe topless right there. So I did the same thing. I took off my shirt and bra. Let the breeze off the Mediterranean brush my upturned breasts as I laid back and drank in the warm sun. It felt so good. I felt beautiful. I felt no shame or embarrassment about my body.

An American man came by to set up a place to lie out, and when he saw the three topless women. he stopped. He just stood there smiling for a moment. He seemed genuinely surprised and pleased. His long look at me, the other women and me again, felt good. Not because a man was admiring my body but because a person was enjoying women, like the works of art and beauty that we are.

I bought a pair of Italian sunglasses. How could I not? They were round and too small and didn't actually fit my face, but who cares. They were heavy and dark, and Italian. Expensive.

There were rumors of a bus that stopped near a cave with tours of the underground formations below the cliffs shaping the Liguria region. Grotte di Borgio Verezzi. A large cave system. It would be a reasonable day trip, both in time and cost. A very quick bus ride and a short walk.

As I approached the entrance where a curly-haired middle-aged woman was reading what appeared to be a steamy Italian romance novel behind the ticket counter, I realized that my timing was terrible. A tour had just entered the cave, and the next one wouldn't begin for almost three hours. Siesta time kept thwarting me, forcing me to slow down. Usually not a bad thing, but there was literally nothing to do but wait here.

The cave was isolated, far from the beaches in town. The road abutted a rocky shoreline that did not appear walkable at all, and there were no businesses. The only thing to do was sit under some trees and wait. I didn't even have any water with me. Totally unprepared. What was I thinking? I must've hung my head down low and started to shuffle away when a friendly young man approached me, jogging up behind, breathless.

"You didn't want the tour with the children anyway! There were too many of them. I will give you a private tour, just you and me. Very private."

Mauricio's eager smile in Rome flashed before my eyes.

Here I was in a foreign land, no witnesses, thinking about entering a large cave system we could get lost in, with another Italian man who could be a rapist or a mugger, for all I knew. Am I going to do this twice?

He watched me think it through, smiling. "I am very good. I give you a great tour, better than any group tour. No kids. Just you and me. Nobody gets that. How special, right?"

I asked how much, and that sent him happily skipping along toward the lady sitting on a wooden stool, reading. They looked alike; I wondered if this was a family affair. "One more for the

12:00, senora." She charged me without even looking up from her paperback.

Ticket in hand, I followed him into the yawning mouth of the cavern. He skipped inside. Youthful energy, or plenty of espresso? I was a little jealous.

"We'll go this way. There is more here to see, but it's very delicate. You make me a promise. I will go on the other side of the ropes, but you will not. No touching, except by me. I am trained, I can only touch the formations, not you. Capisce?"

Capisce, rolling up my sleeves so I could relish the cool, damp air on my skin as we walked. He laughed. He bounded around pointing out various formations and explaining how they were created. He called it a grotte. Grotte di Borgio Verezzi. "The most colorful caves in Italy!" And he was the most colorful tour guide as well, with his white jeans, lime green polo shirt, and checkered Vans.

My eyes were still adjusting, but I began to see his point. "These underground caves, or caverns, are bigger than your Mammoth Cave. Maybe older, but we can only prove it through stories. But we think yes. Once upon a time, that's how you say it, yes? Once upon a time, there were many floods in the region, and one of the local governments decided to do something about it." He was practicing his English, too, and the art of exaggeration.

He paused to step over a red rope, like the kind you see at theaters, hung between waist-high poles. He continued, "There were floods because there were cracks in the rocks."

"Are you going to say the Felsputzers came??" I asked, excited.

"The what? No. I have no idea. No. The workers made the cracks bigger to let water out in certain areas, and when they did this, they discovered a well. Then they ran out of money. Listen."

He flicked his fingers gently on a stalactite. Ting.

I got shivers, what a delightful tiny little sound. If Tinkerbell's wings made a tiny little plucking sound, like the tiniest violin strings or a miniature harp, they would sound a bit like this. Rock made of spun sugar. This was another moment I will never forget – hearing the sound a stalactite makes.

The caves are made of minerals, karst. Red, white, and blue, pink and crystal. Each with its own sound.

"Running out of money, so Italian, right. So later, after they got more money, they kept digging but didn't go far enough to know what was here. See this? It's a room." He gestured to a darkened passageway. "We can't go there, not safe, but it's a room of more formations. FINALLY, in the '50's some cave scientists, uh, we call them spelunkers. They came here and found all the rooms and tunnels and halls we know about today."

I asked if all the rooms and tunnels were known, had everything been discovered now?

"I hope not. We can still dream until we know there's nothing to dream about, yes?"

Yes.

For the next half hour or so, this young man took me through the caves, pointing out various features, giving me a private concert where it was safe to do so. Closing his eyes before gently tapping the delicate stalactites, sliding his finger down toward the fat bases of stalagmites, drumming the cave floor with his fingers as the echoes chased each other into the open cave. He told me to close my eyes to hear better. But then he locked eyes with me as he reached up and rubbed a smooth spot on the ceiling with his palm, as you would a cat's belly. His smile pure and full of pleasure for both sensation and the lack of it, sound and the lack of it. Movement, and the lack of it.

His passion for this underground world was so genuine, so deep. He loves it.

*Please don't do this at home, folks. My tour guide was an expert about this particular place, and its place in time. This delightful memory is mixed with some environmental guilt, but no harm was done. And it's another brief, unexpected moment of magic on this once in a lifetime trip. You can use the Internet to look up videos of cave sounds, including the Cave Organ in Virginia's Luray Caverns. Try searching for the phrase "listen to stalactites."

The night before I left Finale Ligure for San Remo, I heard voices overhead as I walked through the hostel-castle's front gate. It sounded like the voices were coming from the rook at the top of the castle. You can go up there?? Someone has!

I snooped around until I found the tiny dark brick stairwell and headed up it to a pale light and some relaxed American voices. Boys, and one girl – Ginny. They were all sharing a bottle of wine, telling stories, laughing, enjoying the breeze from high above the Mediterranean.

We greeted one another, I joined them briefly. I kept sneaking off to take in the view again as the sun and stars turned the evening into night. They offered me wine. It was clear the boys were preening, competing wildly for Ginny's attention – like the humpback whales I'd one day watch near Puerto Vallarta. A spring ritual.

That next morning, I spent a very long time in the courtyard. I so hated to leave.

And then I went down to the beach to have one last cappuccino in a little porcelain espresso mug.

San Remo

After that last cappuccino on the beach, I left Finale Ligure and went to San Remo in search of a barista I'd gotten to know in Austin while I was finishing school. She told me she'd be working in the shipyards, and that I could stay with her whenever I showed up. So off I went, looking for the young American in the shipyards, with nothing but her first name and a description of her. No luck. I found a small commercial shipyard of dilapidated boats, most in dry dock. Few men were there, repairing them. No women. Not much activity, no sound. Like an undersea graveyard brought aground.

I walked back to town. I had a not very good lasagna for lunch but there was a nice view of the marina. The menu had schnitzel! The Germans come here too, like Finale Ligure. I found an albergo off the Via Roma – it was kind of intimidating trying to find a place to stay without any help from my guidebook. San Remo was not listed there. And there was no hostel that I knew of. I wandered through an ivy-covered outdoor market, called a friend at home to check in, and finally went to the little albergo I'd found. It was a pensione, a small hotel built in a large ancient-seeming building with many flights of stairs, each level a different business.

I once again loved that no one in the entire world knew where I was.

The albergo was lovely. Old, impossibly high ceilings, long thick green drapery pulled back with large, tasseled ropes. Old carpets, old, patched walls. Like you'd see in an artsy movie, an old building in poor repair but still much loved by the proprietress and her son who seemed to be repairing one of the walls as I stepped inside. They clearly lived in this place. She took great pride in helping me hobble along on my foot. She acted like a mama playing nurse, which was weird at first, but then comforting. She propped my foot up with pillows, iced it, bandaged it, kept me eating all evening – no matter how full I was, she kept bringing bread and pasta and eggplant, home-cooked meals you couldn't get anywhere else - until I fell into a truly delicious, long hibernation. In someone's home, in San Remo, Italy.

After tipping my hostess as well as I could, I hopped the train and headed to Nice. My final destination, less one small day trip. I pulled myself up the train's steps, bending a bit to distribute all the weight of my backpack so I didn't fall off backwards, and looked for a seat or empty car.

"Chris!"

No way! SOMEBODY knows where I am!

It was the boys, and Ginny. They were still swarming, she was still the center of attention, and they were inviting me to join them. How cool is that? I did, and we realized that Ginny and I were both headed to Nice. I think it was she who suggested we go to the same hostel, maybe share a room or some meals, which we did. I really wanted to try the fried rice with egg street food I'd read about somewhere, and my new friend was a foodie. So, at the beach in France, she kindly obliged.

But before that, a brief moment of terror. I don't like rule breaking, or at least I don't like the consequences. But I broke a rule without realizing it. I was so excited to see people I recognized that I forgot to punch my Eurail pass. So I got a ticket. Was able to pay in cash, fortunately, as I had very little left on me at the time. 100 French francs. With inflation, I'd guess that's about $25 or $30 now. A lot, but not so much considering how many times I've remembered that terrifying moment getting a ticket in a foreign country from a grumpy uniformed man who didn't speak English. Money well spent.

Nice

Ginny and I made it to Nice, leaving the boys on the train headed to wherever they were headed. Ginny had a place in mind, and we checked in. Nice, clean, cool, but the rooms were larger with multiple beds in them. No worries though, we were going to spend our time out seeing the city anyway. She had a list of places she wanted to visit, including some gardens. I only wanted to get back to the beach. To explore the town a little, but mostly to just be at the beach and take a small side trip to Monaco if I had time.

We did our own thing during the days but came together in the evenings to share what we'd seen that day. She was a seasoned traveler, someone who knew where she was headed in life, what she wanted. Though, when you're young, you don't really know all the twists and turns you'll encounter. Neither of us did. I'm glad we became pen pals, and later social media connections, and I'm glad she's out there in the world as I type this. The world needs more genuine, kind, thoughtful people, and she's one of them.

I went to the beach first. Of course! I watched couples make out, I watched the water. It was a little bluer and the crests a little whiter than they had been in Finale Ligure. There was more sun, or was it that the land was flatter and there were fewer shadows? I walked, I sat, I took pictures. I watched a jet ski competition. Everything, I watched.

I spent a number of days in Nice. I'd arrived there early, so as to be near my departure airport at the end of the trip.

Monaco

Ignoring warnings about pending train strikes, I ran off to Monaco the next day. I wanted to see the casinos, the money, the manicured hills. Grace Kelly's home. But I knew I wasn't dressed for the casinos, and I hadn't the cash.

What I did have was time, and passion for the sea. I went straight to the Musee Oceanographique, Monaco or, as I liked to think of it, the Jacques Cousteau museum. Jacques Cousteau had been here, in this building! What a beautiful building, perched high atop a cliff, pumping water directly from the Mediterranean sea into the aquarium tanks throughout the building.

In the main room of the museum, there was a fin whale skeleton hung overhead. So big you could fit a car in its rib cage. I wrote in my notes that it was harpooned by the HH Prince of Albert I of Monaco and drifted ashore in Pietra Ligure in September 1896.

Whale skeletons look like dinosaur fish.

I saw skeletons of killer whales – "no testimony indicates that killer whales have ever attacked humans."

Thousands and thousands of fish and plants. Living and not. There were fish preserved in water. Oxystomus – serpens (Cannes, 1954), starfish, huge lobster, crabs, little octopuses, the tiny suction cups were little pasta-like circles.

There were intricate fans carved into mollusk bivalves. From Tibet, the Indies, Bengal – seashells covered in silver and gold and gems. Ritual trumpets.

So many treasures. I could've stayed in the museum for weeks.

In the sea-fed aquarium tanks were piranhas, sturgeons, coral taken from Djibouti, and my all-time favorite, the Hippocampe moucheté – seahorses!

Little sea monsters! Such magical little beings. Seahorses wrap their tails around plants to stop floating. Or, when they want to move up in the water, they use the fan-like fins on their backs which act like little motors.

The museum brought the underwater world above-ground. I wish I could have seen the underwater world in the wild, like Cousteau did on his deep sea dives. Or from inside the small submarine sitting outside the museum. I brought home a copy of the Guide to the Oceanographic Museum Monaco (1996) which I have treasured and dreamed with and loved ever since.

After the museum, I went to the marina for lunch. In the marina that day was a Greenpeace ship. I walked to it, around all the yachts and the high-end shops, to a not-so-delicious pasta lunch. The waiter told me Greenpeace was there to replenish supplies before heading out again, and I just sat there thinking about them and their work and all the things that deserve and need preserving in the delicate ocean. I had just seen so many of those things in the past few hours.

Afterwards I walked upward, into the hills. There must've been a staircase. I walked up and up and up and found myself lost in a maze of manicured spiral streets. Every few feet on the concrete there was a white spray-painted symbol of a poodle near a storm drain. The poodles were circled and crossed as if to say, "don't let your dog squat here." I guess you could call them the no poop poodles. If I lived there, spent all that money to live in one of these beautiful homes on one of these beautiful streets above this beautiful sea, I would utterly hate the no poop poodles. HATE.

I got so lost I couldn't find my way back down to the town, to the train station, to sea level. Eventually I spied some American Mormon missionaries going door to door. Even here, in Monaco, they were thrumming up business. I knew what I was doing when I caved in and exchanged my mailing address with them in exchange for directions back down. They wrote to me for years, even though I moved often.

I began reading Virginia Woolf's *A Room of One's Own*. I bought it at a little indie book shop not far from the oceanographic museum. Some women with strong U.S. Southern accents had been there when I walked in. Big women, big floppy hats, big purses, big Alabama accents.

"Excuuuse me, you got any books about Grace Kelly?" Kelly pronounced as if swallowing the end. Kel-leh? GRACE Kel-leh?

The bookwoman did and pointed them to a whole rack. "In enGH-Lesh?" the loud one asked.

The bookkeeper sighed.

Snarkily, she said no, you are in Monaco, we do not carry books about her in English.

The women were appalled. They stormed out, angry and tittering.

It didn't take me long to find what I wanted. I approached the counter slowly, shyly, with my English book in hand, "Bonjour!" I tried, cheerfully. Badly, but cheerfully. She greeted me kindly.

At least I tried. That's all people want, you know. Just try.

Nice Again

"…it is fatal for anyone who writes to think of their sex."

Virginia Woolf, *A Room of One's Own*

A *Room of One's Own*. I'd had no clue what it was about but wanted to read more Woolf. It was small and fit in both my backpack and my budget. What a little treasure. I still have it now, in 2023.

From my journal: "The word "womynism" came to me as I read. Like feminism but womyn (no men). It seems now I have a term for that culture of women, usually gay, that bother me so. Womyn are in danger of repeating history – only it's men that lose this time (no, I hadn't read Atwood yet!). To destroy patriarchal society, which I do loathe, actually means what? To gain power, someone must be defeated. It isn't right. There's still hatred, just reverse. Victimization, struggle for power. How, though, can genuine equality – if that's what we really seek – how can it be had without the ebb and flow of hatred, anger, suppression? To reach balance, the extremes usually must be at least touched.

Men once excluded women from education, the work force, etc. We vote now (I had no idea then how recently we couldn't vote, nor how recently we couldn't have our own bank accounts or property). Today is better compared to that. Yet wages are still not equal. There's still discrimination and prejudice and sexism. But I think if we simply prove ourselves, work for honor, distinction, wages, RESPECT, we have the tools in 1997 to be individuals without hatred, without belittlement, anger or exclusion of men. It's totally unnecessary. But like Woolf says I must belittle YOU to claim my own superiority and power. I must belittle the man, the breeders, the Christians, the normies, the uneducated sheep (excuse me, masses). Okay, I do it too. What groups do I feel superior to? Anyone NOT ME!"

Today we would use the term "out group."

I went on in my journal and wrote: "But must I belittle them? I don't exclude all the 'others' in my list from my life, but I do avoid others. Then I realized – that's why people can be so mean, like the girls looking down their noses at me at the beach in Nice. I do it too. But why? Why are we like that?

I spent a lot of time just sauntering along the Promenade des Anglais, the almost 200-year-old, 5 mile long, raised concrete walkway hugging the beaches. I watched the waves a lot, my eyes and head and lungs filling with blue water and blue sky and fresh oxygenated air. There were plenty of people to watch – lovers making out on the rocky beaches, jet skiers competing for some prize near the sandier shores. There were families walking, cycling, rollerblading… I'd always wanted to try that. So I did.

The rollerblades I rented across the road at a small rental shop were brand new. I was warned it would be hard to stop, that the stoppers in the front of the skates weren't worn in yet. No problem. I hear you. I used to skate as a kid, and I'm not going to go fast anyway.

What a delightful afternoon I had, blading in the sun. Stopping periodically (mostly by gripping rails, to be honest), smoking, gliding. Time stood still and sped up all at once. When the hour neared to return the blades, I noticed that the road between me and the rental shop was going to be a challenge. From my side, I would skate up a small incline. Then halfway across the road, it would go down, down to the curb and sidewalk on the other side. It was the down I worried about, and rightly so.

I couldn't slow down once I started. I steered myself toward a big light pole and tried to grab it but had to simultaneously hop the curb to get out of traffic's way.

I missed. Well, I slowed myself, but I still ended up on my back, on my tailbone. People ran to me from various nearby shops, helped me up, helped me check in with myself. Helped me collect the pieces of my broken Italian sunglasses. Three days, that's all they lasted.

I felt ok except for the tailbone, which wasn't a bad enough injury to call up for emergency medical care or anything. I thanked them all, returned the skates, retrieved my shoes and ID, and went back to the hotel I had moved to.

It was a long damn walk, let me tell you. Every step, my tailbone hurt more. Rest would help, right? No. I couldn't get comfortable, I had more and more pain overnight. I didn't know how or where to get pain pills. So I just suffered. That was ok. My flight home was coming up and I'd just rest until then.

I'll never forget how free I felt, gliding along the Mediterranean, light breeze whipping through my hair, passing people on their own recreational outings, sun on my skin. I loved it.

I haven't mentioned the hotel yet. OMG. After Ginny left Nice, I decided to relocate to an area closer to the public transportation I'd end up using to get to the airport. I also thought just being alone might be nice. There were cheap offerings, and I chose one. It was painted blue everywhere. Every wall, every ceiling, every railing, the same drab blue. Carpet too. The woman who ran the place wore a Mumu and was festooned with flowers. She explained that there was a bidet in the room, but otherwise I'd be sharing the small public restroom with the other tenants on the same floor. When I got to the room, I was a little taken aback. It was filthy, the bed was lumpy and mildewed, but it was mine alone and I could lie down and try to recover my back and tailbone before my upcoming long ass flight.

I was still reading Woolf. Between reading that amazing little book and enjoying the beach, I found myself wanting to take things in slowly, more than letting them out. I had a hard time saying good-bye to the ocean. I'd walk away crying, and then go back and talk to her some more.

We played tag, the ocean and I. She got me good! Splash! I stood there before her, honoring her beauty and power and strength and constancy. She has been caressing and beating and lashing the shore since the earth cooled. She never stops. Ever.

With each crest, she breathes. The rolling motion of the sea is the rise and fall of her rib cage as she inhales and exhales the wind. The sun may set, the wind may cease, she won't. Ever. Her powerful music: crashing waves, followed by a soft gentle rolling when the waters retreat. They lap the shore. She whispers to me.

God is androgynous but the ocean is a woman.

Leaving

Time to go. I hated to leave, though thoughts of a private shower and a good bed and a little Austin cuisine really had started to enter my mind. I would go back to Austin and decide what the rest of my life would look like.

I dragged my aching ass to the airport, checked in a couple hours early. Waited nervously.

There was a family arguing in one of the waiting areas nearby. She was wearing a colorful hijab. There was an older man and a younger man, both angry with raised voices and pointing arms at one another. They spoke another language. There was no telling what they were arguing about, but it was loud, and it went on for a long time. Eventually, the older man took the woman by the elbow and steered her down the concourse. The younger man stormed off in the other direction.

But they left an empty bag sitting conspicuously where they'd been arguing. The next thing I knew, the entire airport was being evacuated.

We were outside standing around, waiting to find out what would happen to our flights. The businessman next to me leaned over, "It was a test. They were testing how long it takes the authorities to find the bag and respond to it. Happens all the time."

Turns out the bag was empty – no bomb. The airport reopened, and all was well. At least on this day it was.

If distance makes the heart grow fonder, I should've been thrilled to return home to Texas. But I couldn't see my future. I couldn't see a path forward, and I had come back home with myself in tow. Home, I didn't even have that – all my stuff was in storage.

A wise friend once said of her own travels, "wherever I go, I go too." There's the rub, yes. I was still drifting, still directionless. Who was I growing up to be? How would I spend my future?

Did I have a book in me?

It was time to find out.

Made in the USA
Middletown, DE
15 May 2024

54400033R00080